T5-CSA-530

PUBLISHED FOR THE MALONE SOCIETY
BY MANCHESTER UNIVERSITY PRESS

Altrincham Street, Manchester M1 7JA, UK
and Room 400, 175 Fifth Avenue, New York, NY 10010, USA
www.manchesteruniversitypress.co.uk

British Library Cataloguing-in-Publication Data
A catalogue record for this book is available from the British Library

Library of Congress Cataloging-in-Publication Data applied for

ISBN 978-1-5261-1392-4

Typeset by New Leaf Design, Scarborough, North Yorkshire

Printed by in the UK by Henry Ling Limited, at the Dorset Press, Dorchester, DT1 1HD

THE TWICE CHANG'D FRIAR

THE MALONE SOCIETY
REPRINTS, VOL. 184
2017

This edition of *The Twice Chang'd Friar* has been prepared by Siobhan Keenan and checked by John Jowett. Completion of the edition was facilitated by a British Academy/Leverhulme Small Research Grant and a Theatre for Society Research Small Grant, for which the editor expresses her thanks. The editor also wishes to thank the following for their assistance with the edition: Kirsten Inglis, John Jowett, M. J. Kidnie, David Morley, Martin Wiggins, and David Hogkinson and Robert Pitt at Warwickshire County Record Office. The editor is also indebted to the previous work on the play by the late Trevor Howard-Hill.

The Malone Society is grateful to Lord Daventry of Arbury Hall for permission to reproduce the play, preserved within Arbury Hall MS A414, and two images from the original manuscript (Plates 1 and 3). Thanks are also due to Warwickshire County Record Office for permission to reproduce images from their microfilm of the play (Plates 2, 4 and 5).

May 2017 JOHN JOWETT

CONTENTS

LIST OF PLATES

INTRODUCTION

The Twice Chang'd Friar is one of four early seventeenth-century manuscript plays bound together in a manuscript miscellany in the library of the Newdigate family of Arbury Hall, Nuneaton (Arbury MS A414).[1] It is the only one of the plays to be prefaced by a title and, as far as we know, this is the only extant copy of the text. The present volume makes the play available in print for the first time. The family was unable to locate the volume within the Arbury Hall library when this edition was being compiled. Fortunately, a draft transcription based on the original manuscript had already been prepared by the editor. This transcription has been checked against photographs of the microfilm of the manuscript held at Warwickshire County Record Office.[2]

The Twice Chang'd Friar is an Italianate city comedy and was first discussed in print in 1906 in an anonymous article in *The Gentleman's Magazine*; fresh attention was drawn to the play in two groundbreaking articles on the Arbury Hall dramas by Trevor Howard-Hill in the 1980s.[3] Like one of the other Arbury plays, *Ghismonda and Guiscardo*, *The Twice Chang'd Friar* borrows its plot from Boccaccio's *Decameron* (published in an English translation for the first time in 1620)—indeed, it is based on the tale that follows the source for the Arbury *Ghismonda* play—adapting the second novella of the fourth day.[4] As Howard-Hill notes, this novella tells the story of Albert, 'a hypocritical friar who gains access to the hitherto faithful Lisetta', wife of Caquirino, a merchant, by pretending to be 'the incarnation of Cupid'. In the play, Albert's plot is eventually uncovered by Lisetta's brothers, but he 'escapes dire punishment by disguising himself with the skin of a great bear'.[5] As well as turning to the *Decameron* for the plot of his play, the Newdigate playwright borrows most of his characters' names from Boccaccio's work. While

[1] Hereafter references to Arbury Hall MS A414 will be cited in the text and will use the continuous folio numbers introduced into the manuscript by archivists at Warwickshire County Record Office (hereafter WCRO). Numbers given in square brackets relate to original numbering on the play manuscript. For further information on the presentation of the play text, see the section 'Editorial Conventions' below.

[2] I am grateful to Kirsten Inglis for sharing her images of the manuscript with me and to WCRO for preparing photographs of their microfilm of Arbury MS A414 to facilitate the checking of my transcription of the play.

[3] See '"The twice chang'd friar. A comedie": (MS. Temp. Charles I)', *The Gentleman's Magazine*, 300 (1906), 285–90; T. H. Howard-Hill, 'Boccaccio, *Ghismonda* and Its Foul Papers, *Glausamond*', *Renaissance Papers* (1980), 19–28 and T. H. Howard-Hill, 'Another Warwickshire Playwright: John Newdigate of Arbury', *Renaissance Papers* (1988), 51–62. My work on *The Twice Chang'd Friar* was inspired by, and is indebted to, the research of T. H. Howard-Hill.

[4] In 'Boccaccio, *Ghismonda*, and its Foul Papers, *Glausamond*', Howard-Hill describes Newdigate's use of Boccaccio's *Decameron* as a source for the *Ghismonda and Guiscardo* play found in Arbury MS A414 and for the playwright's earlier draft of the same play which Howard-Hill entitles *Glausamond* (see WCRO, CR136/B766). Howard-Hill argues that the later version of the play found in Arbury MS A414 was written after, and borrows from, the English translation of *The Decameron*, printed in 1620, whereas the earlier version of the play does not appear to draw on the 1620 translation. Howard-Hill, 'Boccaccio', p. 25.

[5] Howard-Hill, 'Playwright', p. 53.

Albert, Lisetta, and her husband Caquirino take their names from the story of Albert and Lisetta, other characters' names come from elsewhere in the *Decameron*, including Bergamino, Rinaldo, Landolpho, Ricciardo, Dianora, Oretta, Zeppa, and Adrian.[6] Indeed, the only character not to take her name from the *Decameron* is Obedience, Lisetta's waiting woman.

Although set in Venice, the play incorporates several references to London, as a city akin to Venice (see e.g. ll. 1821–4), as well as a series of allusions to England and various aspects of contemporary English life (including the classes of noblemen, knights, and esquires, ll. 1932–3), suggesting that the play's satire (e.g. of courtiers and women) is aimed as much at London and England as at Boccaccio's Venice. Indeed, there is even some direct satire of the English, as when the play's quick-witted courtesans Dianora and Oretta mock an Englishman sent to Italy by his father 'to learn to be / a statesman' for being badly dressed and easily tricked by them at the card game gleek (see ll. 1497–514). The English are mocked, likewise, elsewhere for being changeable and subject to the whims of fashion. Asked to report on the news sent from abroad by his master, Rinaldo describes how, unlike the Dutch who are praised for keeping their 'ancient fashion & state' (l. 1481), the Italians 'change' their fashions 'as oft as haberdashers / doe their blocks, & so are counted apes like Englishmen' (ll. 1482–3).There is also a bawdy allusion to Queen Elizabeth I's infamous royal favourite and important Warwickshire landowner Robert Dudley, Earl of Leicester, with Rinaldo quipping that he might need the assistance of 'My Lo: of Lecesters water' if he is to have an erection and consummate his wedding night with Obedience (l. 2554). This joke borrows from a story included in a controversial satire of Leicester (first published in 1584) which alleged that Dudley kept a special Italian ointment which enabled him to 'move his flesh at all times', as well as 'a bottel for his bedehead, of ten Pounds the Pinte to the same effect'.[7]

The 'Englishness' of the play's Venice is even more apparent in the characterization of the clown figure, Zeppa, who ends up tricking Albert into donning the bear skin disguise in the play's concluding act. His Italianate name aside, Zeppa's portrayal belongs to the long dramatic tradition of English peasant clowns. As well as giving him a regional English accent and having him use dialect words associated with the midlands and northern English dialects—such as 'feck' (l. 2190), meaning by 'the greater part' and 'mun' (l. 2191), meaning 'must'[8]—the playwright laces Zeppa's dialogue with allusions to English country life and traditions.[9] This

[6] See *The Decameron containing An hundred pleasant Nouels* (London, 1620), I, pp. 22r, 31r, 37v, 74r; II, pp. 3r, p. 86r, p. 124r, p. 153r.

[7] *The Copie of a Leter, Wryten By A Master of Arte of Cambridge To His Friend in London* (Paris, 1584), p. 39. The Newdigate Family papers include a manuscript copy of this satire on Leicester (later republished as *Leicester's Commonwealth*) (Arbury Hall MS 5201).

[8] See the definition of the two words in the *Oxford English Dictionary*, http://www.oed.com/.

[9] Zeppa's regional accent is suggested through the spelling used in his speeches. This includes 'much' being represented as 'mich', 'clothes' as 'cloes', 'time' as 'tine', 'knight' as 'kneeght', and 'home' as 'whome' (see e.g. ll. 2176, 2190, 2195, 2240).

includes mentioning his wife's appointment as 'tripe scraper' by 'm^{r} warden' (ll. 2340, 2339) and his son's role as a 'furrier' and 'tanner / of cunnieskins' (ll. 2320–1). Although funny, Zeppa is sharp, too, ensuring that he profits most from Albert's plight, taking money off him for the disguise with which he provides the friar, and money from Lisetta's brothers for facilitating the friar's subsequent humiliation and exposure while in his bear disguise.

Provenance

Arbury MS A414 belongs to Newdigate descendant Lord Daventry of Arbury Hall, Nuneaton, and appears to have been held at the hall since it was first bound at some point in the early eighteenth century. Only some of the material incorporated in the manuscript is dated, but the latest date given is 1702, indicating that the volume's compilation post-dates this year.[10] Although there is no direct proof that *The Twice Chang'd Friar* and the other works included in Arbury MS A414 were part of the Newdigate library prior to their collection in the miscellany, there is plenty of evidence to link Arbury MS A414 and its contents with the early seventeenth-century Newdigate family. This includes the incorporation within the miscellany of a poem which Newdigate family historian Vivienne Larminie attributes to John Newdigate III (1600–42)—'To a Poet whose m^{ris} was painted' (fol. 70r)—the family's ownership of an earlier manuscript version of *Ghismonda and Guiscardo*, one of the other plays found in Arbury MS A414, and the convincing case made by Kirsten Inglis and Boyda Johnstone for John Newdigate III's transcription and authorship of all four Arbury plays (see the section 'Authorship' below).[11]

Physical Description

Paper and Watermarks

Arbury MS A414 has a plain binding of coarse blue-green paper boards and calf, and measures approximately 165mm by 212mm (including the spine). The spine has five raised bands and, at the head and foot, two flatter bands,

[10] The earliest dated text is from 1617 (on fols. 1r–12v); and the latest texts, dated 1702, appear on fols. 38r–49v and fol. 69r. For evidence that the volume was at Arbury Hall in the period following its compilation, see Siobhan Keenan, ed., *The Emperor's Favourite*, Malone Society Reprints, vol. 174 (Manchester, 2010), p. viii.

[11] On John Newdigate III's authorship of 'To a Poet whose m^{ris} was painted' (Arbury MS A414, fol. 70r), see Vivienne Larminie, *Wealth, Kinship and Culture: The Seventeenth-Century Newdigates of Arbury and Their World* (Woodbridge, 1995), p. 173. The earlier manuscript version of *Ghismonda and Guiscardo* is preserved in the Newdigate Family Papers at WCRO (CR136/B766). In this version the lovers have different names: Glausamond and Fidelia. On John Newdigate's authorship of the Arbury plays, see Kirsten Inglis and Boyda Johnstone, '"The Pen looks to be canoniz'd": John Newdigate, Author and Scribe', *Early Theatre*, 14:2 (2011), 27–62.

with 'MSS. MISCI' in the first panel, within a frame of silver or gold ink. Like the other texts bound in Arbury MS A414, *The Twice Chang'd Friar* is written on paper. The miscellany contains 229 leaves, plus two blank uncut leaves at both the front and the back of the volume. The title page of *The Twice Chang'd Friar* occurs on fol. 196r and the text of the play appears on fols. 196v–229v. Original folio numbers in ink appear on each recto from fol. 197r; the numbering starts at '2' and finishes at '34'.

The same quarto volume contains three other early seventeenth-century manuscript plays, as mentioned above—*Ghismonda and Guiscardo* (fols. 77r–102v), *The Humorous Magistrate* (fols. 104r–143r), and *The Emperor's Favourite* (fols. 145r–194r)—and a variety of other early modern texts. The individual manuscripts bound together in Arbury MS A414 vary slightly in size, but the pages on which *The Twice Chang'd Friar* are written measure approximately 145mm by 202mm. As M. J. Kidnie notes, the play may have been collected with the two preceding plays (*The Humorous Magistrate* and *The Emperor's Favourite*) as 'an independent unit prior to the creation of the existing manuscript collection', as these three plays are separated from the first play (*Ghismonda and Guiscardo*) 'by a leaf, blank on the verso, on which is written the word "Plays" in the upper right corner'.[12]

The Twice Chang'd Friar is mostly written in a dark-brown ink. The main exception is the title page which is written in black ink, suggesting that it may have been written later. The text of the play is written on sheets of paper that were probably originally gathered in half sheets; but the fragile nature of the binding of the volume prevented the establishment of the exact gathering of the leaves. The pages on which the play is written are marked by horizontal chain lines, roughly 25mm apart, and the top or bottom of a pot and crescent watermark is visible on several leaves, including fols. 196r [1], 199r [4], 200r [5], 207r [12], 208r [13], 209r [14], 210r [15], 211r [16], 212r [17], 219r [24], 220r [25], 221r [26], 222r [27], 223r [28], and 224r [29].

The play is mainly in English, although there is some use of Latin in the text (see ll. 885, 889, 926, 1531, 2672, 2675–6) and in the stage directions. It is divided into five acts and prefaced on fol. 196v/1v by a list of '*The names of the Speakers*' (l. 4) and '*Women Speakers*' (l. 14) and a '*Prologue*' (ll. 20–41) (see Plate 1); it closes with an '*Epilogue*' (ll. 2697–710). The prologue and epilogue are both written in rhyming couplets. Rhyming couplets also appear at the ends of Acts 2, 3, and 5 and at the end of the first scene of action in Act 4 (see ll. 749–50, 1236–7, 1344–5, 2694–5). The opening title of each act is generally centred, as is the stage direction for the first characters to appear in the scene. The end of each act is marked by another centralized direction. This is usually abbreviated (e.g. '*Fin: Act. 2.*', l. 751). No scene divisions are marked.

[12] M. J. Kidnie, 'Near Neighbours: Another Early Seventeenth-Century Manuscript Copy of *The Humorous Magistrate*', *English Manuscript Studies, 1100–1700*, 13 (2007), 187–211 (p. 197).

Speech prefixes occur in the left-hand margin and are generally abbreviated. The left margin is typically very straight but there does not appear to be any evidence of the paper having been folded to create this margin. Stage directions are usually placed to the right of the page next to the dialogue. Sometimes they are divided from the dialogue by a left bracket or an ink-drawn box (or partial box) around them (see Plate 2). The fact that they are sometimes squeezed in and written over several lines suggests that some of them were written after the text (see e.g. ll. 616–18, 619–21, 2498, 2615–17), although there is also evidence of some directions being written concurrently with the dialogue. On fol. 221r [26], for example, the interlining of the final word of line 1976 ('cloak') suggests that the stage direction at the end of line 1975 ('*puts of / his habit*', ll. 1975–6) was written and boxed before line 1976 was written. Similarly, the stage direction embedded in line 2183 ('*shewes mony*') was implicitly written at the same time as the line in which it appears.

Act divisions, entry and exit directions, and other stage directions are generally written in italic. Directions for the opening and closure of acts and for some exits use Latin, as noted above (e.g. the closure of an act is generally announced by 'Fin.'; collective exits are generally identified by an abbreviation of the direction 'Ex: Omnes', and the exit of a pair of characters is sometimes marked with 'Ex: Ambœ'); otherwise the stage directions are written in English.

Hand

The dialogue is generally written in an easily legible secretary hand, while act references, stage directions, and proper names are typically written in italic, although the author sometimes mixes secretary and italic letter forms in the text and within individual words. This includes using alternate forms of certain letters in the dialogue, such as *e*, which appears in two secretary forms as well as in italic *e* form.[13] Another characteristic feature of the scribe's hand is a tendency to misplace the dot above *i*, frequently placing it high and to the right of the character with the result that a word such as 'times' (l. 75) initially appears to read as 'tmies'. Punctuation is light, but the writer makes use of commas, semi-colons, colons, question marks, exclamation marks, parentheses, and periods. On fol. 228r [33] the scribe also uses a less common combination of punctuation marks: ':://.' (l. 2597). A similar combination of virgules and dots appears in the Arbury versions of *Ghismonda and Guiscardo* (fol. 82r [4]) and *The Emperor's Favourite* (fol. 193r [47]) and a later manuscript version of *The Humorous Magistrate*, preserved in the University of Calgary Special Collections and known as the Osborne version of the play, having previously belonged to the collection

[13] Italics are also generally used for proper names in the dialogue.

of Edgar Osborne (MS C132.27, fol. 4r).[14] It is not entirely clear what the symbol denotes. It could just be a line filler, but Paul L. Faber's research has shown that the symbol resembles one used in musical notation to signal that a section of music is to be repeated (:||:), with the italicized version of the symbol occurring in at least one early modern musical text to denote 'textual repetition', as noted in my introduction to *The Emperor's Favourite*.[15] Given the Newdigates' well-documented interest in music, it is possible that the scribe borrowed the musical symbol, using it as a means of indicating that the preceding word or phrase of dialogue is to be repeated.[16] This might make sense in *The Twice Chang'd Friar*, where the symbol follows the repetition of the command 'Hy Harry Hy' (l. 2597), spoken to Albert disguised as a bear, and could indicate that the playwright expected the speaker to repeat the command several further times, until Albert/the bear '*stands*' (l. 2598).

The manuscript appears to be a fair copy of the play, containing few deletions, corrections, or insertions. The main transcription difficulties the play manuscript poses are a result of the poor quality of the paper, with the text on some leaves being partially obscured by the show-through of text from the other side. Most of the revisions are minor and appear to have been made *currente calamo*, in the same hand and dark-brown ink as the rest of the play. However, there are some occasions where the corrections are in a darker, blacker ink (of the kind used for the play's title page), although the hand still appears to be the same as that used for the rest of the play (see e.g. the notes on ll. 6, 1287, 1444). In these cases, it is possible that the revisions were made later, after the completion of the initial transcription.[17] Line 2606 also affords evidence of a later revision, implicitly having been made after the completion of the relevant stage direction and its boxing, the revised text extending beyond the original ink box around the direction.

Text for deletion is generally smeared or crossed out with a horizontal ink line, with the corrected word(s) inserted above (where appropriate). The main exception occurs on fol. 228v [33v] (see Plate 2) where the writer deletes seven lines of dialogue at the foot of the leaf using a series of criss-crossing ink lines (ll. 2646–52). Inserted text is generally written just above or below the relevant letter or word, often above a caret. On one occasion additional

[14] The Osborne and Arbury versions of *The Humorous Magistrate* were edited for the Malone Society in 2011: Jacqueline Jenkins and Mary Polito, eds, *The Humorous Magistrate* (Osborne), Malone Society Reprints, vol. 178 (2011) (Manchester, 2012); M. J. Kidnie, *The Humorous Magistrate* (Arbury), Malone Society Reprints, vol. 177 (2011) (Manchester, 2012).

[15] Keenan, *The Emperor's Favourite*, p. xii.

[16] Paul L. Faber, 'Crosswords: Textual and Thematic Similarities in *The Humorous Magistrate* and *The Emperor's Favourite*' (Conference of the Humanities and Social Sciences, University of British Columbia, May 2008), pp. 1–9 (p. 3). My thanks must go to Mary Polito for drawing my attention to this research and to Paul Faber for kindly sharing his paper with me. For information on John Newdigate III's interest in music, see Larminie, *Wealth, Kinship and Culture*, p. 114.

[17] One of the revisions made in darker ink is to the name of Caquirino's servant. Initially named 'Rinaldo', his name is amended in the list of '*names of the Speakers*' (l. 4) to 'Reignaldo'. His name is also changed to 'Reignaldo' in the speech prefixes before ll. 51 and 67 but the reviser does not go on to amend the character's name elsewhere in the manuscript.

material is treated differently: an extended insertion of five lines on fol. 226v [31v] is added at the head of the page (see Plate 3). The scribe prefaces the addition with a distinctive trefoil symbol resembling a 'j' topped by three circles; the same symbol is used to identify where the text should be inserted in the dialogue below. In this edition the addition is shown in the place where it was written in the manuscript, rather than in the intended place of insertion (see ll. 2451a–e).

Most of the revisions add or correct individual letters or words only. There are, for example, several instances where a word or words are interlined at the end of a line because the writer has run out of space (e.g. ll. 167, 1798), and there are occasional deletions of mistakes (see e.g. l. 107) and false starts (e.g. ll. 429, 2035, 2486). In at least some cases, the false starts appear to be the result of eye-skip and point to the text being a fair copy or transcription of an earlier version of the play. In several cases, this involves starting a word on one line and then deleting it and putting it at the start of the next line (e.g. ll. 685–6, 2167–8). There are also two instances where the author appears to have made a more sustained false start, transcribing several lines in the wrong place. The first example of this is on fol. 201r [6], where two and half lines of text are deleted (ll. 387–9) and then repeated later, presumably in the correct position (ll. 392–4). The extended deletion on fol. 228v [33v] (ll. 2646–52), mentioned above, also appears to be a false start, with Landolpho's accusation of Albert and Rinaldo's supporting comment apparently being transcribed too early and therefore deleted currently and relocated to the next page (ll. 2658–63).

Although the manuscript is implicitly a fair copy of an earlier text of the play there is some evidence of the author making minor revisions as he copied out the play, replacing individual words and phrases, as in l. 1444 where the more appropriate word 'Sent' is added in the left margin to replace 'feele': 'My Nostrills still / Sent ~~feele~~ yor obseruance to me' (ll. 1443–4). Similarly, he revises ll. 1580–2, changing the grammatical construction of the first part of the sentence and replacing the general word 'time' with the more specific term 'howres': 'No Dayes shall ~~not~~ pass / Nor minutes whose particular expence / Of ~~time~~ ‸ \howres/ doth make them be denominate / The prodigall vnthrifts of vnrecalled time' (ll. 1580–3).

Marginal Annotations

There is evidence of the manuscript being marked up after composition, as there is a series of markings in the left-hand margin in what appears to be a slightly darker ink. Mostly these markings consist of vertical or oblique ink lines (sometimes crossed), but there are also curved lines, inverted commas, a crude pointing hand symbol, and small ink crosses.[18] There are also some marginal annotations: 'not this' or 'not y^{is}' is written in the left margin more

[18] All marginal markings and annotations are reproduced alongside the text in this edition.

than twenty times (see Plate 4 for an example) (ll. 776–82, 836–42, 849–55, 1250–1, 1377–8, 1429, 1497–8, 1632–3, 1690, 1738–9, 1757–8, 1772, 1836–8, 1867–8, 1886–7, 1918, 1978–9, 2013, 2115–16, 2126, 2321–2, 2343, 2553, 2688); 'not transcribed' occurs twice (ll. 1158–60, 1245) (see Plate 5 for an example); and 'Hacten^{s}', a Latin word meaning 'to this place' or 'thus far', occurs once (l. 2196). The handwriting in the annotations is not well-formed but the marginal words appear to be in the same hand as the main text. They suggest that the manuscript was being used to prepare another transcription or version of the play; this other copy of the play does not appear to have survived. Although we cannot be certain of their significance it is possible that the 'not this' annotations identify material which was not to be (or which had not been) copied or transcribed, while the word 'Hacten^{us}' could mean that the text had been (or was going to be) copied out or transcribed up to this point.

The purpose of the various other marginal markings (such as the ink lines and crosses) is less clear, although they, too, could relate to the copying of the play, identifying material for transcription, revision, or omission. It is also less certain whether they were made by the scribe or another reader of the text. In some cases, the markings appear to identify sententious statements, as on fol. 197v [2v] where an ink cross appears in the margin next to the lines: 'Kings & great men reward wth promises / And what they doe must be most exemplary' (ll. 91–2). In other cases, they mark potentially controversial satirical or topical material and thus could signal suggested cuts or censorship, as on fol. 203r [8] where an ink cross appears next to the assertion that 'there's not a yong Lord among a thousand / That knowes an oth^{r} Idiom but sweareing' (ll. 521–2); another ink cross appears in the margin next to Oretta's bawdy suggestion that Lisetta might cuckold her husband '& merit by it, so it be by the instigation / Of an holy broth^{r}' (ll. 590–1). In most instances, however, the purpose of the marginal markings on the play manuscript is unclear, although they—like the annotations—point to the play being read after composition and transcription.

Authorship

Although the four plays found in Arbury MS A414 are unsigned they are of the same penmanship and are similar in their layout and presentation.[19] Parallels include their division into five acts; the use of similar abbreviations for the opening and closure of each act; the use of similar stage directions for entries and exits; and the presentation of stage directions to the right-hand of the page, boxed or marked off by left brackets or ruled lines. Trevor Howard-Hill first made the case for John Newdigate III's transcription and authorship of the four plays in 1988. My own research for my Malone Society edition of *The Emperor's Favourite* lent weight to this authorial and

[19] See Howard-Hill, 'Playwright', pp. 58–9.

scribal attribution, but extensive subsequent research by Kirsten Inglis and Boyda Johnstone has allowed them to confirm that all four Arbury plays are in Newdigate's hand and to make a 'confident attribution' of their authorship to him.[20]

As well as the parallels in handwriting between the plays and other documents in Newdigate's handwriting that Inglis and Johnstone catalogue, there is additional evidence to link Newdigate with the plays, and *The Twice Chang'd Friar* specifically. This includes the use of the distinctive editorial 'j'-like symbol which marks the place of insertion for the five extra lines added at the top of fol. 226v [31v] in *The Twice Chang'd Friar* and for inserted pieces of text in *Ghismonda and Guiscardo* (Arbury MS A414, fol. 94r), *The Emperor's Favourite* (Arbury MS A414, fol. 185r [39]), the poem 'To a Poet whose m^ris^ was painted' (Arbury MS A414, fol. 70r), and Newdigate's 1628 Parliamentary Diary.[21] The crude hand symbol that occurs twice in the margin of *The Twice Chang'd Friar* (ll. 1020–2, 1184–6) though less distinctive, is, likewise, found in at least two documents written by John Newdigate: his 1628 Parliamentary Diary and a page in his hand in his 1630–1 household accounts.[22] Such palaeographical evidence reinforces Inglis and Johnstone's case for *The Twice Chang'd Friar* being in Newdigate's hand, but does not in itself confirm Newdigate's authorship of the play. However, there is evidence for this, too.

As Trevor Howard-Hill noted in 1988, there are significant links between all four Arbury plays in terms of content and style, as well as in terms of presentation and handwriting.[23] There are, for instance, several parallels between *The Twice Chang'd Friar* and the play which appears to have been written shortly after it, *The Emperor's Favourite* (see the section 'Date' below). Superficially, *The Emperor's Favourite* (which has been established to be an authorial text) is a Roman tragedy, loosely based on material found in Suetonius and Juvenal, but several aspects of the plot and characterization appear to borrow from, and build on, the example of *The Twice Chang'd Friar*.[24] Thus Crispinus, the corrupt court favourite who seeks to seduce the virtuous Lucia and Aurelia in *The Emperor's Favourite*, is very like Friar Albert in his abuse of his power to satisfy his own lusts, while the fact that Crispinus seeks to seduce Lucia while her husband (Rabellius) is abroad recalls Albert's preying upon Lisetta while her husband is away as a Venetian ambassador. Similarly, Lucia's eventual frailty in the face of Crispinus'

[20] See Keenan, *The Emperor's Favourite*, pp. xxv–xxxiii; and Inglis and Johnstone, 'The Pen looks to be canoniz'd', pp. 27–62 (p. 51).

[21] WCRO, John Newdigate's Parliamentary Diary (1628) (hereafter PD), CR136/A1, fol. 63r. See plate VIII (p. lii) in *The Emperor's Favourite* for an image of the relevant page from the Diary.

[22] See WCRO, John Newdigate's PD, CR136/A1, fol. 83v; and WCRO, Newdigate Accounts (1630–1), CR136/B616, fol. 13v. The same marginal hand symbol also occurs in *The Humorous Magistrate* (fol. 116r) and *The Emperor's Favourite* (fol. 190v).

[23] See Howard-Hill, 'Playwright', p. 57.

[24] For a discussion of the evidence for *The Emperor's Favourite* manuscript being an authorial text, see Keenan, *The Emperor's Favourite*, pp. xiii–xxi.

charms recalls Lisetta's sudden transformation from loyal wife of Caquirino to willing lover of Cupid/Albert. In both cases, the 'fall' of the heroine is encouraged by two comically bawdy female companions, the courtesans Dianora and Oretta in *The Twice Chang'd Friar* and Locusta and Theodora in *The Emperor's Favourite*. Such similarities of plot and characterization point to an author reworking dramatic scenarios and character types from his earlier play. They are matched by some linguistic and topical parallels between the two plays; both *The Twice Chang'd Friar* and *The Emperor's Favourite* include words borrowed from local Midlands dialects with which Newdigate is likely to have been familiar—with Zeppa using phrases such as 'feck', as noted above, and Hillario in *The Emperor's Favourite* talking of being 'snept' (fol. 158r [12]), l. 890, a Leicestershire word meaning 'to snap' or 'scold'. Both, likewise, include allusions to controversial court favourite the Duke of Buckingham.[25] Although not conclusive, combined with the evidence of the minor stylistic revisions the play manuscript includes, such connections between *The Twice Chang'd Friar* and the other Arbury plays known to have been written by Newdigate suggest that John III was probably the author (as well as the scribe) of *The Twice Chang'd Friar*.

Newdigate had a keen interest in theatre throughout his adult life. As well as seeing plays as a boy and visiting several London playhouses and buying playbooks as an adult, he composed his own poetry and—we now know—plays.[26] Collectively, the Arbury plays point to a writer with an ambitious and wide-ranging interest in drama, including two tragedies (one Italianate and the other based on classical history) and two comedies (one contemporary and English in its setting and the other set in Italy but indebted to the traditions of London city comedy). Newdigate was clearly influenced by, and responding to, metropolitan theatrical fashions and conventions, including the taste for 'covert criticism' of the contemporary court.[27] Indeed, Newdigate even seems to have envisaged his plays being staged in a similar manner to those written for the professional stage (as is discussed below in the section 'Audience and Performance'). Although there is no evidence that Newdigate's plays did reach the professional stage of his day, Inglis and Johnstone are arguably right, nonetheless, when they suggest that Newdigate's work invites consideration alongside the plays of other 'amateur Caroline dramatists' such as 'John Suckling, Mildmay Fane, and William Cavendish, duke of Newcastle', especially for the insights that they afford into regional theatrical culture and the impact of the professional theatre world and its plays beyond London.[28]

[25] For a discussion of the allusions to Buckingham in *The Twice Chang'd Friar*, see the section on the play's date below; for a discussion of the extended satire of Buckingham in *The Emperor's Favourite*, see the introduction to *The Emperor's Favourite*, pp. xxix–xxx, and Siobhan Keenan, 'Staging Roman History, Stuart Politics, and The Duke of Buckingham: The Example of *The Emperor's Favourite*', *Early Theatre*, 14:2 (2011), 63–103.

[26] For more information on John Newdigate's interest in theatre, see Keenan, *The Emperor's Favourite*, pp. xxvi–xxviii and Larminie, *Wealth, Kinship and Culture*, pp. 169–70.

[27] Larminie, *Wealth, Kinship and Culture*, p. 160.

[28] Inglis and Johnstone, 'The Pen looks to be canoniz'd', p. 50.

DATE

The Twice Chang'd Friar is undated in Arbury MS A414 (as are the other plays in the manuscript), but the play's debt to the 1620 English translation of Boccaccio's *Decameron* gives us a *terminus ad quem* for its composition. John Newdigate III bought a copy of the *Decameron* in 1620–1 and the edition appears to have remained in the Arbury Hall library until 1920 when it was listed in the catalogue of books for sale that year.[29] As well as borrowing most of its characters' names from the *Decameron* and its plot from the second novella on the fourth day (as noted above), *The Twice Chang'd Friar* lifts phrases and words directly from the 1620 English translation. Like Boccaccio's Albert (p. 149v) Newdigate's friar describes how Cupid is 'enamour'd' by Lisetta's 'beauty' (ll. 1125–6), and he suggests that Cupid appear to Lisetta in his shape so that she may enjoy the encounter 'wthout taxation of the world' (l. 1214), repeating almost word for word Albert's justification in the English *Decameron* (there the line is 'without any taxation of the world', p. 150r). Likewise, Newdigate's Albert describes how, while Cupid uses his body, the friar's soul will wander in 'louers paradise' (l. 1222), the same phrase used in the English *Decameron* (p. 150r).

Newdigate does not stick entirely faithfully to his source, though; he chooses to have his Albert adopt the disguise of a bear, rather than the shape of a 'savage' man (the choice preferred by the friar in Boccaccio), possibly in another indirect and unflattering allusion to the Earl of Leicester, whose heraldic symbol was the bear and ragged staff. That an allusion to Leicester was in the author's mind could be confirmed by the fact that the bear cannot stand long, an observation which is given a sexual interpretation by Zeppa (ll. 2600–2) and thus recalls the earlier joke about Lord Leicester's 'water' as a solution for erectile problems (l. 2554). The playwright also adapts the story's ending in a potentially pointed way.[30] Boccaccio's telling of the tale concludes with Albert's death from 'some inflicted punishment' and 'conceite for his open shame', whereas the Arbury play ends with Albert's rescue by his holy brothers and their refusal to condemn or punish his adultery (ll. 2669–77), prompting Landolpho to remark of the friars, 'Yo'u're gods in shew but deuillish fiends in action' (l. 2683).[31] While this choice of ending might partly be a way of preserving the play's comic mode, Albert's escape from severe punishment is also in keeping with the play's consistent equation of Catholicism with corruption, hypocrisy, and lechery. Such anti-Catholic satire was popular and politically (as well as religiously) pointed in Stuart England, as tensions flared between England and its Catholic neighbours, Spain and France, in the late 1620s.

The play would have been similarly topical in its persistent satire of courtiers and court ladies, as when Caquirino's servant, Rinaldo, reports

[29] See Larminie, *Wealth, Kinship and Culture*, pp. 116, 200, and WCRO, M.I. 351/9, 1920 Sales Catalogue.

[30] *Decameron*, p. 152r.

[31] *Decameron*, p. 152v.

that Lisetta's friends have told her that it would be 'courtlike to neg=/lect her husband, & giue a seruant courteous / entertainment' (ll. 217–19). In a culture in which there was growing criticism of the Stuart court such satire was culturally and theatrically fashionable. Indeed, the Arbury playwright's drama might be seen as paralleling 'the anti-court satires and political tragedies that professional playwrights were presenting to select audiences at the Blackfriars' in the Jacobean and Caroline eras.[32]

Other topical internal allusions, likewise, point to a date of composition in the 1620s or early 1630s. These include a reference to 'Currants' (l. 1476) or 'courants' (published newsletters), which were first available in England around 1621, when the *Oxford English Dictionary* records the first use of the word, 'courant';[33] and an allusion, in the past tense, to one-time Spanish ambassador to England, Diego Sarmiento de Acuna, count of Gondomar (l. 1962), who left England in 1622 and died in 1626.[34] As noted above, the play also appears to incorporate several allusions to infamous Stuart royal favourite George Villiers, Duke of Buckingham (ll. 143–68), who was at the height of his fame and notoriety in the mid to late 1620s and was a figure in whom we know Newdigate and his circle were interested.[35] These allusions include a possible reference to the chorus of a libellous ballad about the duke, 'Come heare, Lady Muses, and help mee to sing' (l. 475),[36] and a possible sly reference to the duke's title when Albert is described as having been a 'great beater of bucks' (l. 2604). Although superficially a (sexually suggestive) reference to buck-beating (or the practice of beating dirty clothes in a buck or tub during washing or bleaching), puns on Buckingham's name, and puns which associated him with 'bucks' and hunting were common in contemporary libels, partly because of the duke's association with predatory lust, an association shared with the play's transgressive friar.[37] There is also an implicit and mocking allusion to Buckingham's 'magnificent art collection' at York House, with the play's honest merchant Caquirino critiquing those who seek to make a name for themselves through the collection of art and antiquities, such as 'marble' statues (l. 144) and 'antique' heads 'of brass'

[32] Albert H. Tricomi, *Anticourt Drama in England, 1603–42* (Charlottesville, VA, 1989), p. 63.

[33] See the relevant entry in *Oxford English Dictionary*, http://www.oed.com/.

[34] See Glyn Redworth, 'Sarmiento de Acuna, Diego, count of Gondomar in the Spanish nobility (1567–1626)', *Oxford Dictionary of National Biography* (Oxford, 2004); online edition, October 2006, http://www.oxfordnb.com, accessed 24 May 2015.

[35] See Keenan, 'Staging Roman History, Stuart Politics, and The Duke of Buckingham', 63–103.

[36] For a discussion of this ballad, see Alistair Bellany, 'Singing Libel in Early Stuart England: The Case of the Staines Fiddlers, 1627', *The Huntington Library Quarterly*, 69:1 (2006), 177–93.

[37] See the definition of a 'buck' in *Oxford English Dictionary*, http://www.oed.com/. I am grateful to John Jowett for this point about buck-beating. For some examples of the connection of Buckingham with bucks in contemporary libels, see 'To Buckinghame' (L6) and 'Of British Beasts the Buck is King' (Oiiil2), *Early Stuart Libels*, available at http://earlystuartlibels.net/.

(l. 143), equating such conspicuous displays of wealth with egotistical 'high … rais'd ambition' (l. 133).[38]

While the allusion to 'Currants' suggests that *The Twice Chang'd Friar* was written no earlier than 1621, other topical allusions point to a date of composition in the mid to late 1620s. For example, Ricciardo's seemingly random reference to a 'grasier, who owes an / hundred pound' (ll. 1933–4) could be an allusion to the unsuccessful 'Act to restrain Butchers from grasing of Cattle' (presented to the House of Commons on 19 April 1624).[39] As John Pym recorded in his diary, the 'reason of this bill was that the butchers having many beasts beforehand, make themselves masters of the price both in buying and selling', potentially making it difficult for other graziers to compete with the butchers in the meat marketplace and thus to make a living.[40] The play's allusion to Robert Dudley, Earl of Leicester (noted above) would also have been topical in 1624, the earl having been mentioned in parliament as the first courtier to receive a patent during the Commons' discussion of the long-awaited Statute of Monopolies (passed 25 May 1624).[41] Although John Newdigate did not sit in the 1624 parliament we know that he took a lively interest in national and international politics, and is likely to have been aware of some of the key bills debated.

Other allusions point, however, to a date of composition in the second half of the 1620s. These include an allusion to eating cream at Hyde Park (l. 2430), which became a popular resort among the fashionable London elites, following King Charles's opening of a horse-racing track there around 1628, and a number of satirical references to the French and French fashions (see ll. 1511, 1814, 1893, 1961, 2224, 2227, 2243–4).[42] Anti-French satire—like anti-Catholic satire—flourished in the aftermath of Charles I's controversial marriage to French Catholic Princess Henrietta Maria in 1625 and the declaration of war with France in 1627, as contemporaries worried that Charles and the English church were in danger of conversion to the rival religion. A date of composition in the late 1620s might also explain Zeppa's cryptic comparison of Albert to one of the gentlemen 'that went the last voyage' who 'made him so / good cloes to loose his blood in, yet he thought they / were too braue to be killd in, & therefore when he / saw there was any daunger, he made him selfe a free / pass wth his heeles & run away' (ll. 2197–201). The English were involved in several embarrassing military operations during

[38] Roger Lockyer, *Buckingham: The Life and Political Career of George Villiers, First Duke of Buckingham, 1592–1628* (London, 1984), p. 409.

[39] 'House of Commons Journal Volume 1: 19 April 1624', in *Journal of the House of Commons, vol. 1: 1547–1629* (London, 1802), *British History Online*, http://www.british-history.ac.uk/commons-jrnl/vol1/19-april-1624, accessed 16 February 2017. I am grateful to John Jowett for this suggestion.

[40] '19th April 1624', in *Proceedings in Parliament 1624: The House of Commons*, ed. Philip Baker (2015), *British History Online*, http://www.british-history.ac.uk/no-series/proceedings-1624-parl/apr-19, accessed 17 February 2017.

[41] See the Diary of John Pym, '20th April 1624', in *Proceedings in Parliament 1624*. I am grateful to John Jowett for this point.

[42] Alec Tweedie, *Hyde Park: Its History and Romance* (London, 1930), p. 67.

the early years of Charles I's reign which led to complaints about English cowardice and military unpreparedness. In 1625 the Duke of Buckingham organized a naval expedition to take Cadiz which failed when the English soldiers sent to conquer the city instead got drunk on local wine. In 1627 Buckingham led a similarly ill-fated expedition against the French at the Ile de Ré. This was followed up by two further failed missions to relieve the French Huguenots at La Rochelle in 1628. Many men were lost in these expeditions and Buckingham (as Lord Admiral) was widely blamed, especially for the failures at Cadiz and Ile de Ré, which occurred before his assassination in August 1628. Contemporary satires and libels mocked him as cowardly and better suited to courtly recreations such as dancing and fashion than to military leadership, mockery similar to that Zeppa offers of the unnamed 'gentleman' to whom he likens Albert in the play.[43]

A date of composition in the early Caroline era would make sense, too, in terms of what we know about the order in which the four plays included in Arbury Hall MS A414 appear to have been written. Internal evidence (such as textual echoes and connections between the plays) suggests that *The Twice Chang'd Friar* was the second written of the dramas included in Arbury Hall MS A414, being preceded in date by the other play based on a tale from Boccaccio's *Decameron*—*Ghismonda and Guiscardo* (written *c.*1623–8)—and before the plays known today as *The Emperor's Favourite* (written *c.*1627–32) and *The Humorous Magistrate* (written *c.*1634–7).[44] Indeed, if *The Twice Chang'd Friar* post-dates 1627 (as is possible, given the anti-French satire and the allusion to Hyde Park mentioned above), it potentially narrows the dating of the playwright's next play—*The Emperor's Favourite* (*c.*1629–32)—and increases the likelihood that *The Twice Chang'd Friar* was written in the late 1620s (*c.*1627–30).[45]

[43] On the Cadiz and Ile de Ré expeditions see e.g. Tim Harris, *Rebellion: Britain's First Stuart Kings* (Oxford, 2015), pp. 245, 260–1; on the libelling of Buckingham in the aftermath of these humiliating military defeats, see e.g. 'And art return'd againe with all thy faults' (Oii12), *Early Stuart Libels*, available at http://earlystuartlibels.net/ in which the duke is castigated for his 'base ignoble cowardise' (l. 64) and advised to 'stay at court then, and at Tennys play, / Measure French Galliards out, or Kil-a-gray' (ll. 95–6).

[44] For a discussion of the evidence for the order in which the plays were written, see Howard-Hill, 'Another Warwickshire Playwright', pp. 51–6 and Martin Wiggins's entry on the 'Tragedy of Fidelia and Glausamond' in *British Drama, 1553–1642: A Catalogue, Volume VIII* (Oxford, forthcoming). Howard-Hill's research points to 1623 as the earliest date of completion for the Arbury version of *Ghismonda and Guiscardo* ('Playwright', pp. 51–2), while Martin Wiggins's research suggests that the revised version of the play preserved in British Library Additional MS 3412, fols. 139r–186r was probably completed around 1628 and almost certainly after 1627. On the evidence for the dating of *The Emperor's Favourite* and *The Humorous Magistrate*, see Keenan, *The Emperor's Favourite*, p. xxii–iv and Kidnie, *The Humorous Magistrate*, p. xi. I am grateful to Martin Wiggins for sharing his research on the plays with me in advance.

[45] This evidence for the dating of the two plays is in line with Martin Wiggins's 'best guess' dates for their composition: *The Twice Chang'd Friar* (1630); *The Emperor's Favourite* (1632). See Martin Wiggins, *British Drama, 1553–1642: A Catalogue*, Volume VIII (Oxford, forthcoming). *The Twice Chang'd Friar* appears as entry 2317 in Wiggins's catalogue.

There is no record of *The Twice Chang'd Friar* being performed at the time of its composition or since, although an amateur performance at Newdigate's family home (Arbury Hall) or one of his rented houses in Ashted or Croydon could have escaped record. It might be easy to conclude, therefore, that it is one of W. W. Greg's 'closet' dramas, 'never acted' or intended for performance, and yet there are several reasons to believe that Newdigate did write with the possibility—or aspiration—of performance in mind, as noted above.[46] The play is prefaced by a list of '*Speakers*' (l. 4) and '*Women speakers*' (l. 14) (my emphasis) (see Plate 1), rather than by a list of the 'persons of the play', and opens with a prologue in which the 'free born authour' (l. 20) addresses himself to 'selected freinds' (l. 21), but in which he anticipates the presence of others in his audience whom he claims also to have considered in his writing: 'Yet least some other iudgem^{ts} should despaire / They could not vnderstand a word, his care / Hath stoop't to their capacitie, & will / Enfeeble powerfull lines that their low skill / May haue some feeling of 'hem' (ll. 22–6). In its identification of a mixed audience of supporters and would-be critics, this prologue is much like those written for the public playhouse plays in the Jacobean and Caroline eras and suggests that, whether or not it was performed, Newdigate imagined *The Twice Chang'd Friar* enjoying some kind of life beyond his 'closet'. Indeed, it could reveal a playwright with aspirations to see his plays performed, whether privately or semi-privately in his household or more publicly, perhaps even on the professional stage.

That Newdigate envisaged a staged performance is arguably confirmed by the play's epilogue where he alludes to the audience's 'vneasie seats' (l. 2697) and their potentially 'weary' eyes (l. 2707), 'eares & other parts' (l. 2707), and invites them to 'grace the authour' (l. 2710) with their 'applausiue hands' (l. 2709), phrases which imply a seated audience present at a physical performance of the play, rather than an audience of readers. Further evidence that the playwright imagined the play being performed is found in the stage directions. As in the other Arbury plays, the stage directions carefully record the stage properties needed for the action (including a bell, book, candle, confessing chair, garter, gold, money, a sword, tweezers, a bodkin, and the bear skin and visor which Albert wears when disguised and taunted as a bear), as well as directions for the few special effects required, including knocking (ll. 564, 1025, 1868, 1992), bell-ringing (ll. 609–10, 2498), and Friar Albert's appearance '*wounded*' (l. 2161) in Act 5 after being confronted and injured by Lisetta's brothers. The text, likewise, affords some very specific information about the expected costuming of characters. There are, for instance, numerous allusions to the nature of Friar Albert's costume as Cupid, with several characters mentioning that he wears a silver suit with silver wings, 'a quiuer /at his back,

[46] W. W. Greg, *A Bibliography of the English Printed Drama to the Restoration*, Vol. 4 (Oxford, 1959), p. xii.

a scarfe ouer his eyes, & a sword in his hand' (ll. 2252–3). The detail into which Newdigate sometimes goes with his directions might well be 'markers of amateurism', as Inglis and Johnstone note, being at 'odds with the practice of most professional playwrights', but it was not unusual for printed plays to include detailed information about special costumes and effects, and this attention to detail still points to an author thinking carefully about the physical realization of his play.[47] We find evidence of a similar attention to staging and costuming in the work of other amateur dramatists from the period, such as Mildmay Fane, perhaps partly because such authors could not leave such matters to others, as was the case with professional playwrights working for the public theatres. Amateur playwrights who envisaged staging their plays were generally obliged to take responsibility for all aspects of the performance, including properties and costuming.[48]

The playwright consistently marks the entries and exits of characters with stage directions. Like the other Arbury plays, *The Twice Chang'd Friar* also alludes to the use of doors as entry and exit points. At the end of Act 3 scene i the exit of Lisetta's chambermaid, Obedience is followed by the direction '*Enter at the other dore, Albert & Ricciardo*' (l. 986) and at the end of Act 4 scene ii the exit of Oretta is followed by the direction '*Enter* ^*at the other dore,/ Lisetta, & Obedience perfuming*' (l. 1386). Although such references to doors could simply be mimicking the language of printed playhouse plays, they suggest that the playwright was thinking in terms of a staged performance using a playing area backed by two doors, one possibly fitted with a window through which Obedience on one occasion '*lookes out*' (l. 1993) (implicitly from backstage) and '*then returns, speaks*' (l. 1993). Such staging facilities are akin to those available at the public playhouses. The play's action implicitly requires a 'discovery' space of the kind thought to have been available at some of the public playhouses, too: in Act 4 Albert is required to enter '*in his study*' (l. 1703), as is the character of Theophilus in Philip Massinger and Thomas Dekker's *The Virgin Martyr* (printed in 1622), and in Act 5 Lisetta's brothers are at one point required to '*stand aside / hidden*' but implicitly still on the stage (ll. 1923–4).[49]

That the play was 'directed toward performance' as well as, or instead of, reading might also be suggested by the fact that it does not share some of the 'readerly' devices scholars such as Marta Straznicky have identified as being common in those manuscript plays that 'sought to be inscribed

[47] Inglis and Johnstone, 'The Pen looks to be canoniz'd', p. 31. I am grateful to John Jowett for the point about directions in printed plays.

[48] For a discussion of Fane's detailed instructions regarding the 'technical production' of his plays, see Gerald W. Morton, 'Mildmay Fane's Northamptonshire Theatre', *Northamptonshire Past & Present*, 7 (1988), 397–408 (at pp. 400, 401–3). I am grateful to Martin Wiggins for this point.

[49] See Phillip Messenger and Thomas Deker [*sic*], *The Virgin Martir* (London, 1622), sig. K2. I am grateful to John Jowett for this cross-reference.

in literary' rather than performance 'culture'. There is, for instance, no 'introductory argument outlining the context and action of the play', no 'lengthy sententious speeches', nor 'a chorus serving to prompt and guide interpretation'.[50]

The play does not include a theatrical licence from the Master of the Revels, nor does it show clear signs of being marked up for playhouse use (e.g. there are no readying directions for actors' entrances or required properties of the kind found in some of the manuscript playbooks associated with the theatres), but this is perhaps not surprising given that the play's auspices and any performances are likely to have been amateur. That the play is the work of an amateur is also suggested by the fact that there is at least one potential staging problem. It is not clear, for instance, how Albert enters in his study in Act 4 scene v, unless there was a concealed 'discovery space', as noted above. There is also a potential plot problem as there is some ambiguity about how much time is meant to have elapsed between Acts 4 and 5. Act 4 closes with Albert telling Lisetta to prepare for a second visit from Cupid, yet in the opening scene of Act 5 Oretta will claim that Cupid 'often visitts' Lisetta (l. 1854). However, such problems with time schemes are not unknown in plays written for the professional stage, too (there has been much debate, for example, about the timescale in which the events of Shakespeare's *Othello* unfold).

Nonetheless, the fact that *The Twice Chang'd Friar* was annotated after transcription and possibly used as the basis for another copy of the play, could be evidence that the play was being readied for more than reading. Household performances or staged readings would not have been without precedent, as we know from the example of Newdigate's contemporary Sir Edward Dering and the private theatricals organized at his family seat, Surrenden Hall.[51] Newdigate might have hosted similar performances at one of his houses. Arbury Hall would certainly have afforded a number of potential performance venues, such as the Elizabethan Hall and Great Parlour.[52]

Whether or not *The Twice Chang'd Friar* was performed or read aloud as part of a 'staged reading', it is likely to have been shared with others—as is suggested by the evidence of its being copied—and, in that sense, was not a 'private' text confined to the author's 'closet'. John Newdigate regularly shared literature with friends, such as Oxford don, Gilbert Sheldon.[53] Indeed, a marginal note on one of the other Arbury plays (*The Humorous Magistrate*) alluding to a 'Dr S.' (fol. 106r) and reporting, or inviting, his comment on one of the speeches could be a reference to Sheldon. It is

[50] Marta Straznicky, 'Closet Drama', *A Companion to Renaissance Drama*, ed. Arthur F. Kinney (Oxford, 2004), 416–30 (at pp. 417, 422).

[51] See Michael Dobson, *Shakespeare and Amateur Performance: A Cultural History* (Cambridge, 2011), pp. 26–30.

[52] See Geoffrey Tyack, *Warwickshire Country Houses* (Chichester, 1994), pp. 9, 14.

[53] See Larminie, *Wealth, Kinship and Culture*, p. 134.

thus likely that Newdigate shared his plays—including *The Twice Chang'd Friar*—with at least some of his cultural associates. He may have been thinking of such people, and possibly even a particular reader or readers, when annotating the text for transcription (with phrases such as 'not this'). It is presumably to such 'freinds' (l. 21) that Newdigate also alludes and with whom he imagines sharing the play in the prologue and to whom he addresses himself when he apologizes for his theatrical 'ofspring' (l. 2705) in the epilogue.[54]

Editorial Conventions

In this semi-diplomatic edition the following editorial conventions have been observed. Deletions are indicated by striking through the relevant letters: ~~thus~~. Angle brackets enclose text which is illegible or difficult to read (e.g. because of paper damage or show-through); dots indicate illegible characters: <...>. Interlineations inserted above the line in the dialogue are represented within slashes as follows: \thus/. Conversely, interlineations inserted below the line in the dialogue are represented as follows: /thus\. On two occasions the interlined material is so extensive that it has resulted in the line being turned over in this edition (ll. 1248, 2274). In the manuscript some interlineations are preceded by a caret. Where carets are used they are represented in the text at the point where the interlineation needs to be inserted. This does not always match the exact position of the caret in the manuscript, in which case the actual position is recorded in the textual notes. The position of text interlined in the left margin is reproduced when it does not interfere with the sense of the line. Where stage directions are inserted in the right margin the original position of the material is reproduced in the text.

Original page numbers appear as they do in the play manuscript in the right-hand margin of the transcription space. Later or editorial foliation is given in square brackets further right. Where two numbers are given in square brackets the first number relates to the continuous folio numbers introduced into MS A414 by archivists at Warwickshire County Record Office (WCRO); the second number relates to the original ink numbering system in the play manuscript and is only recorded in this position when it is absent from the manuscript. Original lineation has been preserved as far as possible,

[54] To figure one's writing as one's 'child' (l. 2702) was not uncommon in this period, but might have had an added poignancy for Newdigate, given that he had no surviving children. Newdigate family historian Vivienne Larminie reports that John Newdigate's wife Susanna gave birth to a 'stillborn son', buried at Arbury in 1622 'and probably another in 1623', but the couple were to have no surviving children. It is noteworthy that Newdigate appears to have turned to writing plays after this date. Vivienne Larminie, 'Newdigate, John (1600–1642)', *Oxford Dictionary of National Biography* (Oxford, 2004); online edition, January 2008, http://www.oxforddnb.com/, accessed 9 July 2008.

but the line numbers added in the right margin of this edition are editorial. Each line of text, including deleted lines, act divisions, and stage directions, is numbered separately; the lines are numbered continuously from the title onwards. Speech prefixes (SP), act divisions, and stage directions (SD) are reproduced, as far as possible, as they appear in the manuscript. The playwright does not mark scene divisions. These have been introduced editorially each time that the stage is cleared; they are shown in square brackets.

Newdigate sometimes mixes italic and secretary letter forms in his writing, but speech prefixes and stage directions are generally in italic in the manuscript and are therefore reproduced in italics here. Italics are occasionally used in the dialogue too, mainly for proper names and place names. Where such names are italicized in the dialogue they are also italicized here, although there are some occasions where it has been necessary to use editorial judgement about whether to italicize the relevant words, as Newdigate occasionally mixes secretary and italic forms within them.

Original spelling, punctuation, abbreviations, and contraction signs have been retained. Original capitalization has also been preserved, although determining whether letters are capitalized in words that appear at the start of lines has sometimes been a matter of editorial judgement because Newdigate's majuscule and minuscule forms of characters such as *m*, *n*, *y*, and *w* are almost identical. Newdigate's use of apostrophes to represent contractions varies. Sometimes he does not use apostrophes for contracted word forms, such as *ith* for *in the*. These omissions are preserved in this transcription. Similarly, where apostrophes are used in the manuscript they are reproduced here. Occasionally, instead of using an apostrophe Newdigate leaves a space to mark the omission of letters (e.g. *i th* for *in the*). In each case this edition preserves the presentation of the original manuscript. Where an apostrophe occurs at the end of a word in the manuscript it is generally not followed by a space (e.g. 'th'imployment', l. 109). The original presentation is reproduced in this edition.

There are also variations in Newdigate's handling of prefixes such as *a*- (in words such as *about*) and *in*- (in words such as *instead*); the author occasionally leaves a space between prefix and word. Sometimes the space between the prefix and word is significant, so that they appear to be separate words. Where this occurs, the words are shown separately in this transcription. Similar variations occur in the writer's handling of compound words. Whereas many of them are joined in the manuscript, this is not true of all, especially in the case of the various -*self* compounds (e.g. *myself*, *yourself*). Where such compound words are shown as separate words in the manuscript they are shown as separate in this edition.

The transcription preserves *u* for modern *v* and *i* for *j*, in majuscule and minuscule forms. Superscript letters are represented in superscript form. Thorn is represented by *y* as in y^{is} for *this*. Tildes are represented by a small curved line above the letter preceding the contraction. Long *s* has been replaced by short *s*; and terminal secretary *s*, which can represent a contraction of *es* or *is*, is represented by the symbol ꝰ. The contraction symbol for *pro* is represented in the transcription by *φ*; and the contraction symbol for *per* is represented by *ρ*. The ligature *œ* has been retained. Examples of overwriting and alterations to individual characters and words are recorded in the Textual Notes. Later marginal annotations are distinguished from the main text through the use of a different font.

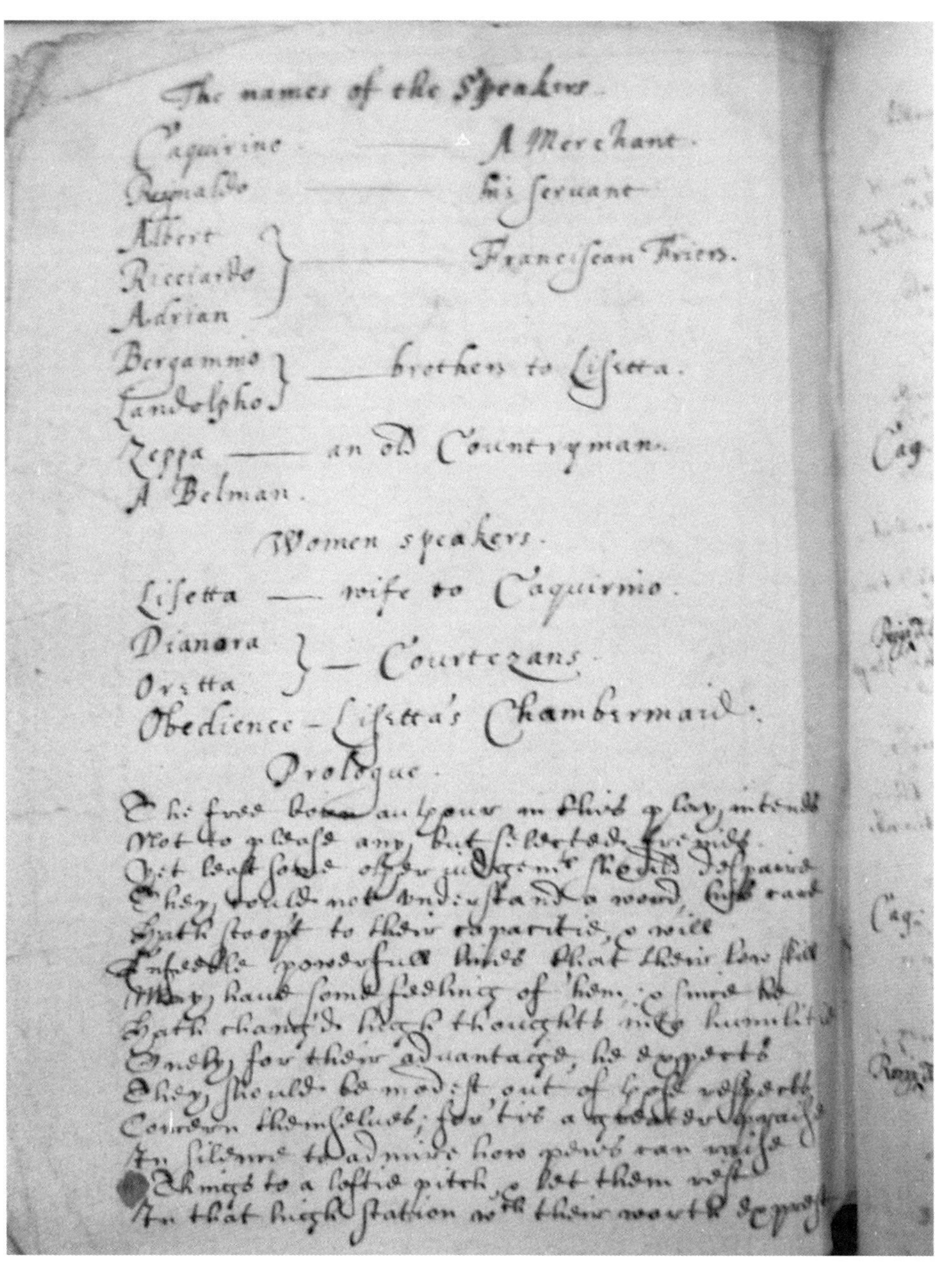

The names of the Speakers.

Caquirino —— A Merchant.
Reynaldo —— his servant.
Albert, Ricciardo, Adrian —— Franciscan Friers.
Bergammo, Landolpho —— brothers to Lissetta.
Zeppa —— an old Countryman.
A Belman.

Women speakers.

Lisetta —— wife to Caquirmio.
Dianora, Oretta —— Courtezans.
Obedience — Lisetta's Chambermaid.

Prologue.

Plate 1: Arbury Hall MS A414, fol. 196v/1v

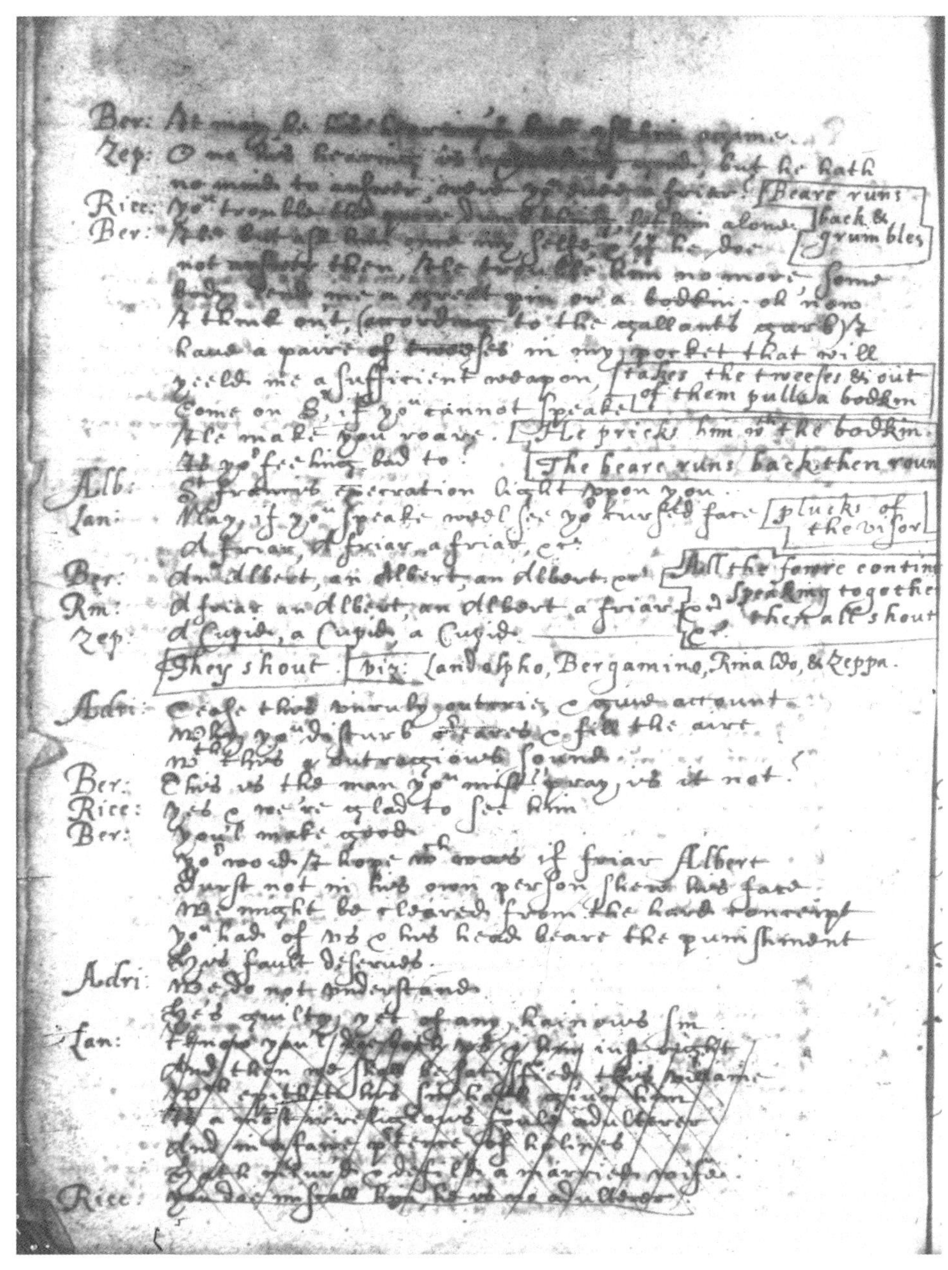

Plate 2: Arbury Hall MS A414, fol. 228v/33v
(Warwickshire County Record Office, M.I. 351/3)

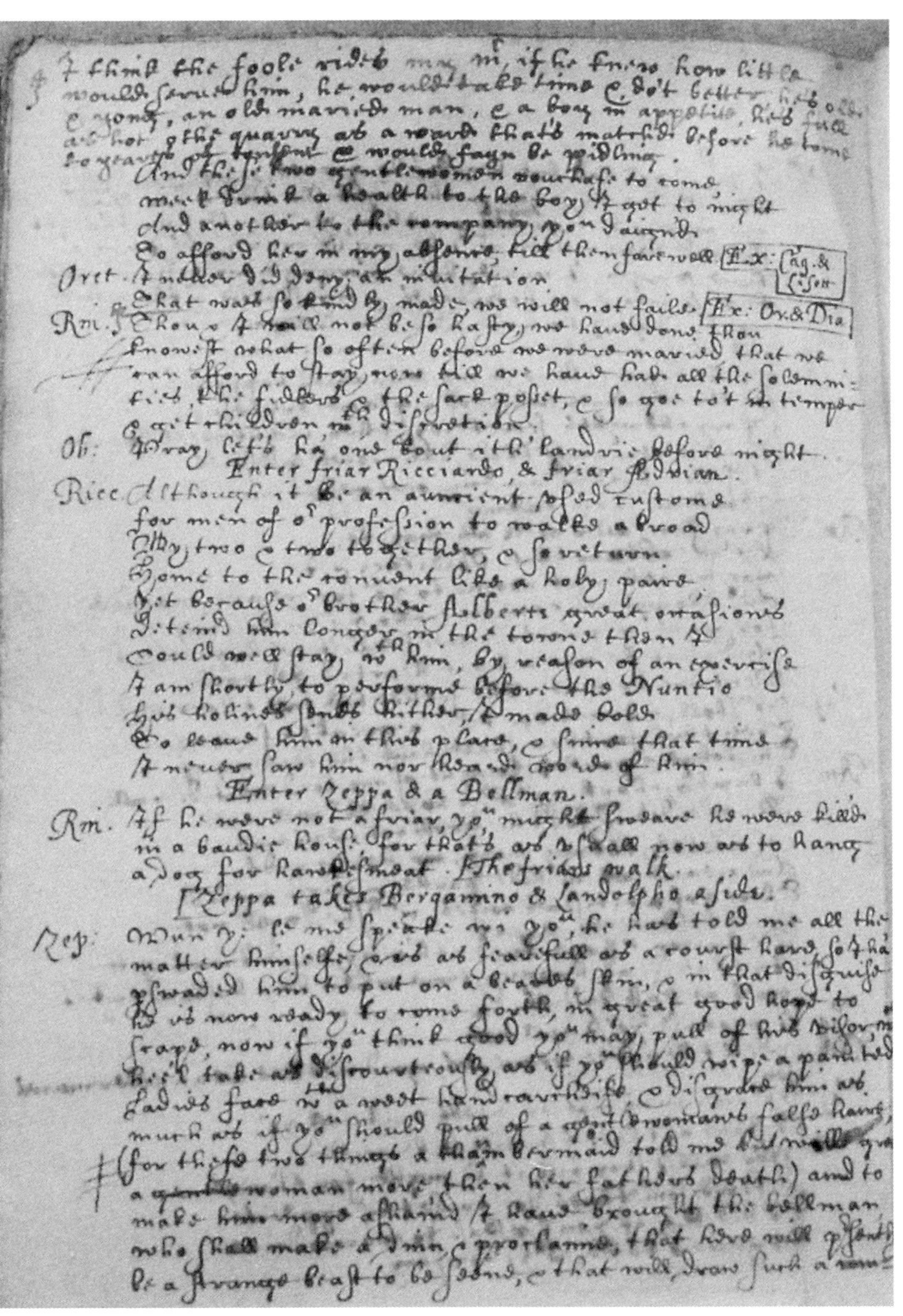

I think the foole rides me, if he knew how little would serve him, he would take time & do't better, hee's old & young, an old married man, & a boy in appetite, hee's full as hot o'the quarry as a rook that's matched before he come to yeares of [illegible] & would fayn be pidling.
And these two gentlewomen vouchsafe to come
meet drink a health to the boy y'got to night
And another to the company, y'ond [illegible]
To afford her in my absence, till then farewell [Ex: Ang. & Lisett]
Orct. Another did deny an invitation
That was so kindly made, we will not faile. [Ex: Or. & Dia.]
Rin. Then I will not be so hasty, we have done thou knowest what so often before we were married, that we can afford to stay, now till we have had all the solemnities, the fiddlers, the sack posset, & so goe to't in temper & get children wth discretion.
Ob: Pray, let's ha' one bout ith' laundrie before night.
Enter friar Ricciardo, & friar Adrian.
Ricc. Although it be an auncient [illegible] custome
for men of or profession to walke abroad
Thus, two & two together, & so returne
Home to the convent like a holy paire
Yet because or brother Alberts great occasions
Deteind him longer in the towne then I
Could well stay wth him, by reason of an exercise
I am shortly to performe before the Nuntio
his holiness sent hither, I made bold
To leave him in this place, & since that time
I never saw him nor heard word of him.
Enter Zeppa & a Bellman.
Rin. If he were not a friar, yor might sweare he were killd in a baudie house, for that's as usuall now as to hang a dog for [illegible] meat. [The friars walk.
[Zeppa takes Bergamino & Landolpho aside.
Zep. Marry [illegible] he me spake wth yor, he has told me all the matter himselfe, & is as fearfull as a course hare, so I ha' pswaded him to put on a beare's skin, & in that disguise he is now ready to come forth, in great good hope to [illegible], now if yor think good yor may pull of his visor, [illegible] he'll take as discourteously as if yor should wipe a painted ladies face wth a wett handkerchiefe & disgrace him as much as if yor should pull of a gentlewoman's false haire, (for these two things a chambermaid told me [illegible] a woman more then her fathers death) and to make him more ashamed I have brought the bellman who shall make a [illegible] & proclaime, that here will presently be a strange beast to be seene, & that will draw such a [illegible]

Plate 3: Arbury Hall MS A414, fol. 226v/31v

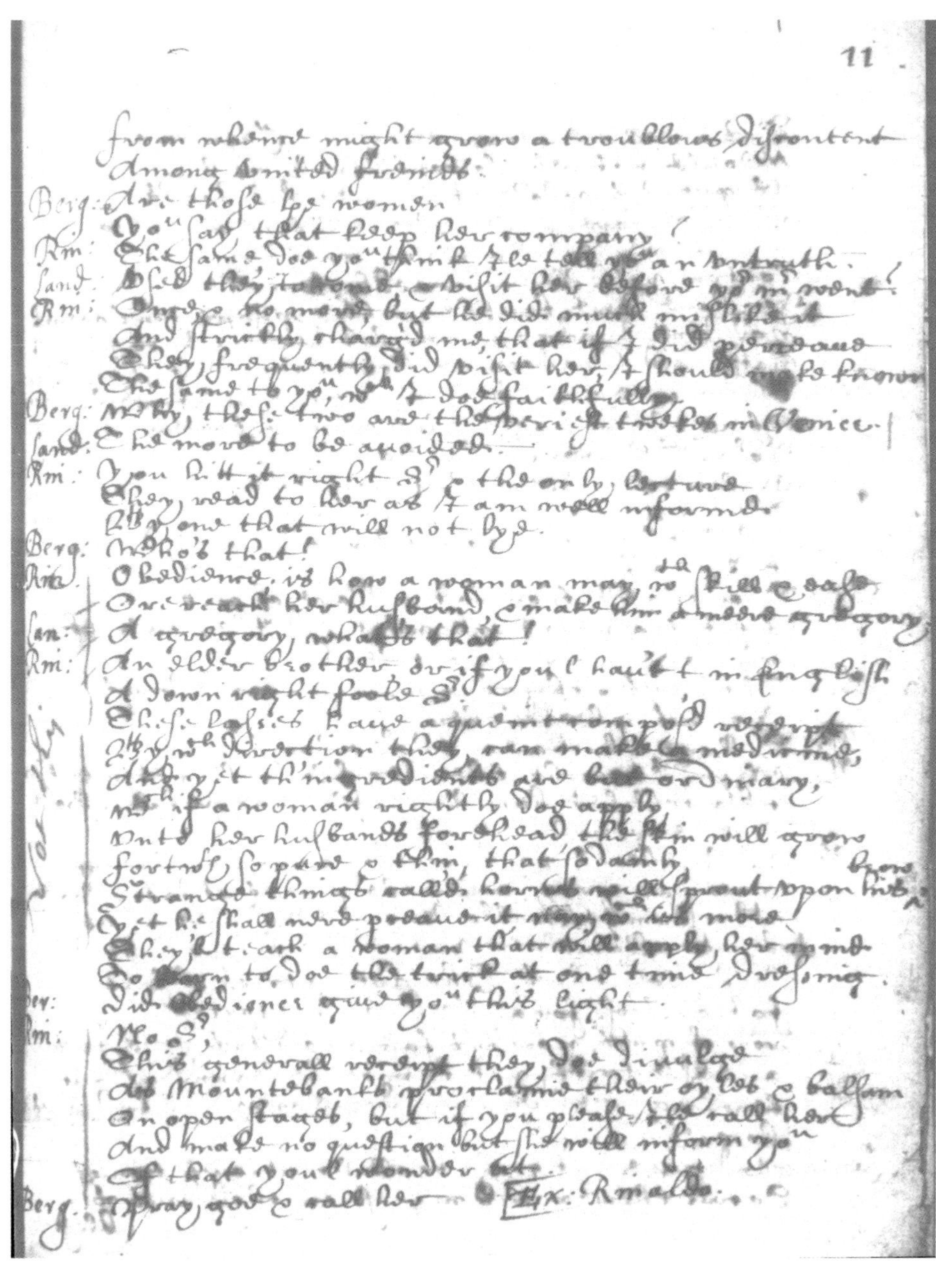

11

from whence might grow a troublous discontent
Among united friends.
Berg: Are those the women
You say that keep her company?
Rin: The same. Doe you think Ile tell you an untruth.
Sand: Used they to come & visit her before you went?
Rin: Onye no more, but he did much mislike it
And strictly charg'd me, that if I did perceave
They frequently did visit her, I should make known
The same to you, wch I doe faithfully.
Berg: Why, those two are the [illegible] in Venice.
Sand: The more to be avoided.
Rin: You hitt it right Sr, & the only lecture
They read to her as I am well informed
By one that will not lye.
Berg: Who's that!
Rin: Obedience, is how a woman may still be safe
Overreach her husband, & make him a meere Gregory
San: A Gregory, what's that!
Rin: An elder brother Sr if you'l have it in English,
A downright foole Sr.
These ladies have a quaint compos'd receipt
By wch direction they can make a medicine,
And yet th' ingredients are but ordinary,
wch if a woman rightly doe apply
Unto her husbands forehead the skin will grow
forthwith so pure & thin, that suddenly
Strange things call'd hornes will sprout upon his brow,
Yet he shall never perceave it nay wch is more
They'l teach a woman that will apply her mind
To learn to doe the trick at one time dressing.
Ber: Did Obedience give you this light
Rin: No Sr,
This generall receipt they doe divulge
As Mountebanks proclaime their oyles & balsam
On open stages, but if you please Ile call her
And make no question but she will inform you
Of that you'l wonder at.
Berg: Pray goe & call her. Ex: Rinaldo.

Plate 4: Arbury Hall MS A414, fol. 206r [11]
(Warwickshire County Record Office, M.I. 351/3)

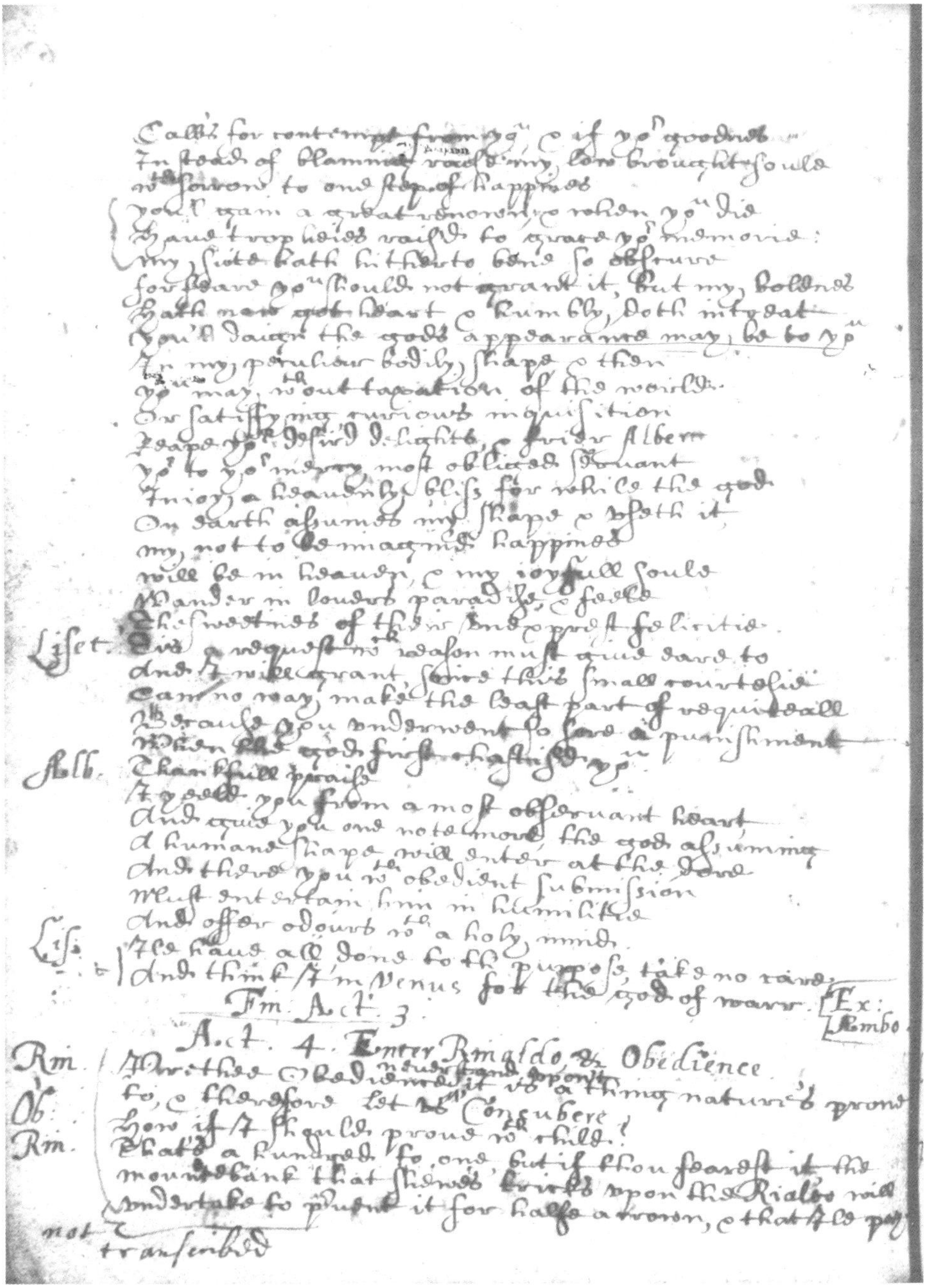

Plate 5: Arbury Hall MS A414, fol. 211v/16v
(Warwickshire County Record Office, M.I. 351/3)

[Fol. 196r/1r]

The twice chang'd Friar. A comedie.

[Fol. 196v/1v]

The names of the Speakers.

Caquirino. — *A Merchant.*
Reignaldo — *his seruant*
Albert, *Ricciardo*, *Adrian* } — *Franciscan Friers.*
Bergamino, *Landolpho* } — *brothers to Lisetta.*
Zeppa — *an old Countryman.*
A Belman.

Women speakers.

Lisetta — *wife to Caquirino.*
Dianora, *Oretta* } — *Courtezans.*
Obedience — *Lisetta's Chambermaid.*

Fol. 196r/1r] title written in black ink Fol. 196v/1v] text written in brown ink that gets darker from here onwards 6 *Reignaldo*] *eig* written over *i* in darker ink 16 *Dianora*] *o* written over *a*

Prologue.

The free born authour in this play intends
Not to please any but selected freinds.
Yet least some other iudgem^{t}c should despaire
They could not vnderstand a word, his care
Hath stoop't to their capacitie, & will
Enfeeble powerfull lines that their low skill
May haue some feeling of 'hem; & since he
Hath chang'd high thoughts into humilitie
Onely for their aduantage, he expects
They should be modest out of those respects
Concern themselues; for 'tis a greater praise
In silence to admire how pens can raise
<T> Things to a loftie pitch, & let them rest
In that high station wch their worth exprest

2 [FOL. 197r]

Their own; then offer to depose a straine
from it's great height, whose braue transcendent ‸\vaine/
Sits on a supreme throne, where their dull eies
Cannot discern it's strong abilities.
His first nam'd freinds, he's confident will beare
Wth this digression, to whom his carefull feare
Bowes, & intreats their liking wch once granted
Will shew, they mist not any thing they wanted.

Act. 1. [Act 1, scene i]

Enter Caguirino, Rinaldo.

Cag. Not that I haue the least cause of distrust
Or make a doubt of thy fidelitie
Take I this strict account, but as thy truth
Hath shew'd it selfe a ready seruitour
Of me & my occasions, so I desire
To satisfie thee by acknowledgement
Of all thy well mean't & perform'd indeauours.

Reig‸\n/aldo. My hitherto spent dayes I should repent
And seriously greeue for, if my conceipt
Were so below the seruice I haue vowed yo^{u}

32 <*T*>] blotted a pen stroke   35 *transcendent* ‸*\vaine/*] caret below ²*t* of *transcendent*   48 *desire*] followed by   51, 67 *Reig*‸ *\n/aldo*] altered from *Rinaldo* in darker ink

As once to force my guilty cheeke to blush
for feare you should mistrust me, seruants are
Their masters raising or their ouerthrow
Especially to men of yor profession,
And if yor iudgem^{t} shall not think I am
As true as you can wish me, please yor selfe
Ether in keeping or reiecting me.

Cag: My approbation in myne own close breast
Hath nam'd thee good & meritorious,
Nor couldst thou haue consum'd thy youthfull dayes
And those since spent in any mans imployment
Who would haue tooke so fatherly a care
Of giuing thee reward.

Reig‸*n*/*aldo*. A happier day
Mine eyes nere saw the light in, nor did I wish
Wthin my priuate thoughts for such applause;
My earnest mind, (iust like a dreaming man
Who when his pleasing phantasie obiects
Something that giues delight, awakes to see

[Fol. 197v / 2v]

Whether his dreame be true, & being awak't
Not sees the same, but some assimilation
Of what the night afforded) hath diuers times
Hop'd to be cheared with a fauouring looke
From yor smooth brow, yet hath some anxious ‸\\feare/
Vpon the sodain so surpris'd my hopes
That what I thought in earnest, sodainly
I fear'd to be a dreame, yor approbation
Hath ta'n of all these doubts, & by a way
Not subiect to deceipt giu'n testimony
Of yor great worth by promising reward
With the free voice of yor vnaltered word,
wch modest expectation nere would suffer
my slow tong to intreat, yor open hand
Scornes to be vrg'd to liberalitie
By this in these dayes often vs'd inforcement.

Cag. My promise shall be m^{r} of my purse

56 *ouerthrow*] *w* possibly altered from *n*

Yet yo^{u} must giue me leaue t' appoint the time
× Kings & great men reward wth promises
And what they doe must be most exemplary
To vs their agents, please thy selfe wth this hope:
For on my word tis a well grounded one.

Rin: I'm infinitely pleasd yet honour'd S^{r}
Some feeling for the p^{r}sent were not amiss,
And as the basis of a piramid
Makes it stand long & firmly, so the least thing
Vouchaf'd in p^{r}sent from yor bounteous hand
Would be a groundwork to futuritie.

Caq: He that goes slow goes sure, & 'tis not safe
To stretch a thing aboue it's vsuall pitch,
Nor must yo^{u} think by ouer hastie meanes
To gaine a prize from me, but moderation
And long expecting temperance acquires
Reward before those heady hot braind men
That think their fathers ~~life~~ ‸\liues/ their ruining;
Yo^{u} know th'imployment I am bound for, and
Cannot be ignorant that the state of Venice
Hath chosen me to goe Embassadour
About th affaire in Flanders, till I return
Take care of what is in yor charge, & put
My stock to gainfull trading, thus yo^{u} shall
Make yor m^{r} bound to you, & more ingage

3 [Fol. 198r]

Me to haue yo^{u} in my thoughts, Call in yor m^{ris}
My farewell for a long time I must take
Of her & then I'm gone *Exit Rinaldo.*
Trusty *Rinaldo*,
Thou hast merited & I will recompence,
Nor will I like a most perfidious statesman
Imploy thee so long, till my own occasions
Be brought to their perfection, & then shake of
Thy seruice & thy selfe, when all thy paines
Should reape the fruit it hitherto ‸\hath/ toild for.
Nor am I niggard of my wealth, because
Herewth I meane to raise a lofty columne

107 *~~life~~* ‸*\liues/*] caret below *e* of *~~life~~* 121 *occasions*] *i* altered 123 *paines*] *s* smeared for deletion

W^{ch} fixed at my studie dore may shew
I built it to perpetuate my fame,
And being inscrib'd wth great siz'd characters
May satisfie th' inquiring passenger
Here *Caquirino* tooke his great account
And here he told his gold, my priuate mind
Aspires not to so high a rais'd ambition.
Such tropheies doe beseeme the man that dare
Seeke ho^{r} a new way, who if he faile
And ill success doe frustrat his designes
Yet hath the happy fate of being esteemd
A noble leader, & the imputation
Of what ill ere succeeds, must be laid on
The meaner props of greatnes, wch could not erre
But by direction from the generall;
He's much deceiu'd that think I hor'd vp wealth
T'imploy this way; no antique head of brass
Nor marble statue can so take my sense
Though I were certaine it bore *Cesars* likenes
That I would barter gold for't, although I know
Great mens conceipts spurr'd on wth an opinion
That if they value highly but a meddall
Stampt in *Augustus* time, the meaner sort
Will think them schollers & great antiquaries,
And being vplifted wth this vaine conceipt
Will buy at any rate an high pris'd relique,
When the great sum̃ perhaps of twenty thousand
Lyes vnpaid at their mercers, & they to win
The vulgars wonder or an heralds praise

[Fol. 198v/3v]

Leaue the poore needie creditour vnpaid
To buy these dustie peeces for their galleries;
W^{ch} though they cannot vnderstand themselues
Their titles being in obscure characters
Will giue a Critick many pounds a yeare
To tell them what a ras'd word signifies;
And when this puft vp pride a while hath swelld

132 *gold*] *d* altered

Iust like a bubble & at length doth breake
They quit the house of Criticks whose applause
Made them spend much because 'twas scholerlike
And run in debt onely to gaine repute,
But I haue found their fate, these men must ‸ \needs/
At length grow beggers ~~by~~ ‸ \for/ their reputation.
Rinaldo. [*Enter Rinaldo.*]
Rin. Doe you call S^{r}?
Cag. Where's yor m^{ris}?
Rin: As close at work as may be, *Dianora*
She & *Oretta* are in disputation,
They are so earnest, speake so thick & loud
That if you were among them yo^{u} would sweare
× Yo^{r} chamber were the womens *Academie*
Caq: *Lisetta* will not come then?
Rin: Yes S^{r} p^{r}sently
And by me doth intreat you'l please to pardon
Her that she stayes so long.
Cag. What's their discourse?
Rin: When I inform'd her yo^{u} desir'd to take
Yo^{r} sad leaue on her, & that p^{r}sently
Cause yor occasions would not ꝑmitt long stay,
Oretta said my m^{ris} was most happy
Because yo^{u} were to goe so long a iourny,
At wch yor kind wife, wth this newes perplext,
Shedding more teares then vttering words, replied,
Those that loue not their husbands think the day
They part in happy, but my loyall heart
Owing more duty, & respectiue loue
To *Caquirino* then th' Egiptian Queene
Braue *Cleopatra* shew'd to *Anthony*
Curse the day that disioynes vs, but *Oretta*
And *Dianora* vrg'd, this kind of absence

4 [Fol. 199r]

Sometimes is most expedient, & affirm'd
A husbands dayly p^{r}sence did ~~s~~too much tie

164 *applause*] a^{2} altered or smeared
168 *~~by~~*] *b* written over *f* or altered to *f*, then deleted
197 *too much*] written over smeared text

The wife to strict obseruance, & did cause
× Her to be bashfull in great company;
When if she had but libertie afforded
To goe abroad though but to see a motion
(I mean such motions as are now most vsuall)
'Twould gaine her husband such a reputation
Among great Ladies, that he should be reputed
The only man deseru'd a Courtlike wife
And one knew how to doe a woman right

Cag: 'Tis a most proper theme & now in vse
'Mong women that disclayme profounder things,
But is *Lisetta* on the right side sayst thou?

Rin: If it be right to seeme to loue her husband.

Caq: To seeme?

Rin: Yes S[r], tis a word of large extent.
For a woman may seeme to loue, & yet loue not, & seeme not to loue, & yet loue most intirely, therefore I beseech yo[u] be not offended, that I said seeme, but this I can assure yo[u], when they did offer to peruert her, & told her 'twas courtlike to neg= lect her husband, & giue a seruant courteous entertainment, she wept & said twas naught, & when they vrged such errours she still held the negatiue.

Cag: A negatiue tenent fitts a woman best.

Rin: Then she's as you would haue her, & holds out stiffe, 'gainst all their allegations, *Oretta* and *Dianora* are the strong opponents, & good *Lisetta* answers, but who do yo[u] think is modera= tour, euen little *Obedience* my m[ris] chamber= maid. *Enter Bergamino, Landolpho, & Lisetta.*

Caq: My dearest wellcome, thou art worth esteeme
Thy modestie reiects inticeing Sirens
And is victorious 'gainst their ill suggestions.
Brothers by information from *Rinaldo*
I vnderstand yo[r] sister & my wife
Hath got the conquest ore the dames of *Venice*

[FOL. 199v/4v]

219 *said*] *i* inserted

Liset Were it not that a stricter obligation
Then most wiues beare in mind had power on me
And that I know the crime's vnexpiable
To slight a womans husband, the inticement
Of *Dianora* & *Oretta* might
Haue soone peruerted a weake womans mind.
Cag: Hold yo^{u} there still *Lisetta*, fame thus got
And kept becomes a femall S^{t} on earth,
'Twill be a comfort when the whistling winds
And troublous seas deny my body rest
To haue my mind in quiet, because thy though<ts>
Not liable to change being thus approu'd
Shall scorn th'assaults cunning hath power ‸\to/ make
Gainst thy chast hold.
Berg: 'Thath bene obseru'd
And 'tis an honour to o^{r} family
That no man euer did select a wife
Out of o^{r} stock or kinred, whose aduerse chance
Repentance shewed he had a cause to greeue for
Except it were because he match'd no sooner.
Land. And 'tis the com̄on fate of all the women
To die before their husbands, there's no man ‸\breath<es>/ ~~breath<..>~~
whose much retaining long liu'd memory
Can contradict this truth, onely one girle
My vnckles daughter maried at fifteene
(Whose heart was farr more tender then her yeares)
Saw her husband die, & sadly following
His much lamented corse to buriall
wth oft fetcht sighes & many teares expir'd
Rin: By yor fauour S^{r} had none of these children
before they died?
Land: Yes many.
Rin: Sons or daughters?
Land: Both
Rin: Of wch sex most?
Land: The children most were girles:

256 ~~*breath*<..>~~] blotted

Rin. 'Thad bene a cursed com̃onwealth els,
for were it not for such a familie
whose kindnes is incomparable, we might die

5. [FOL. 200r]

And die againe before o^{r} courteous wiues
would weepe themselues to death
Berg: The reason as we find it in records
Is giu'n to be this, the first woman
Of the family that was so kind was of the
stock of *Niobe*.
Rin: May not a woman wth the help of onions, & barr
Dying weepe as much?
Berg: But not wth such heart breaking sobs.
Rin: I am of yor mind for that, 'pray be not offended
that I put in a word by the way.
Berg: There's no offence com̃itted
Cag: 'Tis the dutie of a man that's put in trust
To fitt all time & all occasions
Whereby he may the most completely perfect
What he's inioyn'd to doe; yet hath the state
Taken great care, & granted me free licence
To settle all mine own affaires at home
W^{ch} this hower hath accomplisht, for *Rinaldo*
Hath giu'n me an account not to be question'd
Of all was in his charge, wch satisfaction
Hath made me to comitt my whole estate
Into his hands againe, & if it chance
That I return not to see how his care
Doth act it's second part, my deare *Lisetta*
Question him not for any thing is past,
But as yo^{u} find his trust when I am gone
Imploy him in the future.
Liset. No rule binds me
~~*Liset.*~~ So strongly as yor word, & yor iniunction
I prise a boue a written veritie

304 *a boue*] = *aboue*

Caq: All wiues must stoope to thee, & thy obedience
\+ Many will curse, because it giues example
Of what their stiffe necks cannot paralell.
My brother *Bergamino*, & *Landolpho*
'T hath bene the vse for maried womens freinds
To seeke by kind words & faire born indeauours
Onely to gaine the husbands strong affection
Intirely toward his wife, but I that nere
Saw any thing in my deare=lou'd *Lisetta*

[FOL. 200v/5v]

But what did fitt a well deseruing wife
Think I am bound in an obliged tie
Of loue to her, t' intreat both yo^{u} & all
My happy fate hath giuen me interest in,
That when I'm furthest of, & she bereft
Of him should giue her aid, that yor prompt hands
And what els she doth need, & yor com̃and
may wth a ready willingnes indeauour
To doe her all iust right.
Berg: Mine own ingagement
Besides the charge that yo^{u} haue layd vpon vs
for wch we are bound euer to honour yo^{u}
Inioynes me to loue ^ \her/ but since that worth
Appeares in yo^{u}, wch he that emulates
Yet in a farr of distance counterfets
Merits a noble praise, my whole abilitie
Shall serue her, not because she is my sister
But that I know she's *Caquirino*'s wife.
Land: To say as much in various worded termes
would seeme the same, & I but a repeater
Of what my brother said, but since those powers
(Whose ^ \reasons/ ~~powers~~ we must not search but admire)
Haue blest o^{r} ~~powers~~ ^ \house/ wth the felicitie
Of hauing yo^{u} o^{r} brother, though I cannot
Or gratifie yor selfe or yor desert,
Ile charge the strength of my abilitie

305 *thee*] *ee* blotted   335 *reasons*/~~*powers*~~] deletion and insertion in darker ink   336 ~~*powers*~~ *house*/] deletion and insertion in darker ink; caret below *w* of ~~*powers*~~   338 *or*] *r* written below superscript *r*

To be so ready when her needfull sum̃ons
Shall call it to imploym^{t}, that yo^{u} shall know
(When heauen will please that yo^{u} return ~~againe~~ ‸\againe/)
Nature & mariage onely had the power
To name vs brothers but the true affection
My dayly actions still shall manifest
To her, shall giue yo^{u} cause to nominate
Me euer yor true freind.

Cag: This tie is greater
Then can depend on consanguinitie,
And since th' ineuitable vndertaking
The state imposeth on my carefull shoulders
Inioynes my hast, Ile not be prodigall
Of those few minutes in mine own dispose
To question yor not to be question'd loue

6 [Fol. 201r]

Yo^{r} own exp^{r}ssion hauing satisfied
What I can ask or think of. As dying men
Value their last breath most, yet neuer thought
A multitude of howers before mispent,
So I the man whose vndeseruing merit
Had such a heauen afforded priuiledge
As the highly to be prised company
Of such a wife, & th' inexplicable bliss
Of oft conuersing wth a paire of freindly
Brothers or brotherly freinds did not take hold
Of vndisturbed howres, wherein I might
Haue app^{r}hended fully & inioyed
The sweet of these true blessings, but wastfully
As men in youth prise no time but the present
Consum'd those howers, of wch the meditation
Had they bene right imployed, would haue p^{r}serud
Me many yeares wth feeding my content;
But wise men nere inquire a remedie
For things that are past cure, but quietly
Submitting to the sacred will of heauen
Abide it's iust decree; my aduerse fate
And now not to be remedied inforceth me

342 ~~*againe*~~ ‸*againe*/] ~~*againe*~~ blotted or smeared; caret below ^{1}*a* of ~~againe~~   356 *of*] retraced

Kisseth her. To take my greeu'd farewell. My deare *Lisetta*
may the night when thou liest downe to take re=‸\pose/
Be free from any noyse, but that choice sound
The spheres doe make by their quick=turning motion
Vnles it chance some softly murmuring spring
Casting a rill out vnder thy chamber window
make thy closd eyes continue their still posture
Vntill the god of sleep doe ꝑsonate
Me to thy dreaming sense; & when the day
Shall please to barr thee of this kind of rest
~~And it stands wth thy mind to walk abroad~~
~~May no wind stirr but the health bringing gale~~
~~Of *Eurus*, & let that~~
Casting its peircing rayes in at those chinks
Where night flyes out exild by dayes bright ~~<.>~~power

[FOL. 201V/6V]

And it stand wth thy mind to walke abroad,
May no wind stirr but the health=bringing gale
Of *Eurus*, & let that so mildly blow
It may but aire thy cheeke, & by that touch
Draw the pure coloured blood to it's right place
W^{ch} would ascend it selfe but that it knowes
The East wind is ingagd to doe thee seruice.
Kiss again. And so the blest powers still protect thee.

Lisett. A womans thanks
Would but detract from the desert they're sent ‸\to/
Therefore Ile silence words & vtter teares.

Caq. Thy meaning's app^{r}hended, & thy thoughts
I need not know by any more exp^{r}ssion.
Brothers farewell the happines I wish
my selfe abroad, such may betide at home
Both yor known worth.

Berg. 'Twere an vngratefull tong
That should not giue yo^{u} thanks, though emptie ‸\aire/
Sent out of those vnable mouths that can
More wish, then giue yo^{u} furtherance would \bewray/

377 *greeu'd*] *d* possibly altered from *e* and blotted 378 *re=‸\pose/*] caret below = 402 *words*] *wo* altered 411 *\bewray/*] possible caret below, between *h* and *e* of *heart* in l. 412

weakenes in speaking when mine vnknown heart
Thinks bettr to reprsse that facultie,
Vntill some opportune occurrence may
Make my thoughtꝭ known by action, onely this
I cannot cease to vtter, that my prayers
Shall frequently intreat for prosperous gales
To cause yor speedie & most safe returne.

Land. May the to other passengers rough seas
To you be calme & smooth, & *Neptunes* selfe
Take such care of yor waue dissecting ship
As if his hory head did take a pride
To beare it safe vpon his rugged bosome.

Caq: At once I thank you both, brothers, fare‸\well/
Adieu *Lisetta*, often times adieu,
Yor charge *Rinaldo*'s giuen, nor need I vrge
Yor more obseruance. *Ex: Ões pret. Rinaldo.*

Rin. I greeue Sr that I am not

7 [Fol. 202r]

So worthy as yor merit bids me yet ~~since~~
Since yor to be admir'd humilitie
Hath giu'n *Rinaldo* such a large ꝑmission
To gouern all you haue till you return
Ile be as carefull as yor selfe were prsent
And that day take the most delight when I
may raise you wealth by painfull industrie

Finit Act. 1. *Ex*:

Act. 2. *Enter Lisetta, Oretta, & Dianora.* [Act 2, scene i]

Orett. Leaue of this puritanicall reseruednes
For as you are now you are scarce good company
× for a well bred dogg.

Liset: Bereft of that should giue my plesures life
I ioy most in retirednes, & 'twere a sin
for me, who while my husband was at home
Inioy'd as much as woman could desire,
Not to retaine him in my memorie.

Orett. Think on him but be merry.

Lisett. You councell me to contradiction,
Can I be merry when the vnquiet waues
Haue such a treasure in their vnstable keeping

As *Caquirino* is?
Dia: Suppose in ouer louing this sweet man
They so imbrace him in their fomie surges
That one p^{r}sumptuous billow aboue the rest
Doe chance to catch him, & so drown his wor^{pp}.
Liset This supposition is my way to death.
Dia: But if it fall out true, you cannot help it.
Liset. Yet I can greeue for't.
Oret. And what followes then?
Liset. A sad remembrance of his ample merits
Which were so great to me, that should he perish
'Twere not enough to die to disingage
Me of that strong made obligation
W^{ch} my low duty owes his memory
Oret Oh how you liue in erro^{r}, could yor kind heart
Be well content to die for a dull merchant?
Doe yo^{u} think 'twere possible that if for eu^{r}y loss
Great^{r} then this,, (for the loss of a husband

[Fol. 202v/7v]

Is such a little, petty, puny loss)
I should haue wrung my hands & tore my haire
And wash'd my face in brinish fretting teares,
In stead of smoothing water & pomatum,
That euen the meanest magnifico in *Venice*
Would hold me in esteeme?
Liset. I goe a way
Cleane contrary to yo^{u}, & if my care
And strict obseruance to my absent husband
At his return reape but the wisht for fruite
Of his being pleasd; it will be more to me
Then if the greatest man in all the citty
Should bend his knee at my cõmanding beck.
Dia: Is this the way yo^{u} goe?
Liset. Yes & a right way.
Orett. Repent for 'tis a most erroneous way.
Can you giue such obseruance to a thing
That knowes not how to weare his clothes,

467 *this,,*] second comma possibly inserted 469 *haue*] *e* altered

Nor kiss his hand? & when he weares a cloake
He pulls it all before iust like a shepheard.
Liset. My husband's better bred then you imagine,
He hath a dancer that comes euery morning
To teach him how to make a leg.
Oret. What & haue his cloake lined wth serge?
Liset. You are deceiu'd, quite through wth beaten veluet.
for since it pleasd the graue state to take notice
Of his wise head, & call~~d~~ him to imployment,
He hath not wanted any complement
W^{ch} might befitt him in a great mans p^{r}sence
But at his second going to court he made
Him two faire cloakes, the one is lined wth veluet
The other wth rich plush.
Dia: Is his doublet lined wth plush?
Liset. No tis too costly.
× *Oret.* There's no corrupter of women but frugalitie.
Ile not deny but by imployment vnder
The state, yor husband may in time attaine
To a politick garb, & such as may be behoouefull
To the thing he goes about, but 'tis impossible
That if he think it is too much expence
To line his doublet through wth plush or sattin
That he should be a complete gentleman.

8. [Fol. 203r]

I must confess the states vnanswered reason
Cannot be spoke against, since their wise choice
Selects such men, who so they may be call'd
My Lo: Embassadours, will scorn to take their pay.
But vpon their own charge free all expence
Prouided they may haue this emptie name.
'Tis not to be denied, but merchants are
Much fitter men to carry embassies
Then noble men, because by conuersation
wth those of sundry nations they are able
To speake their minds in diuerse languages,
When there's not a yong Lord among a thousand

494 *call~~d~~*] *d* erased 519 *those*] written over *men*

× That knowes an oth^{r} Idiom but sweareing,
And yet Ile vndertake a ruffling Lord
Is worth twenty such, as *Caquirino* ~~is~~
For things about home.
Liset. Yet not so to me:
Oret Peace, & heare reason, if an high com̃ing Lord
Should send ith' morning to know how yo^{u} doe
And if yor liking stand to goe abroad
I th' after noone, he would fetch yo^{u} wth sixe horses
And be yor ready seruant all the while
Yo^{u} please to take the aire, could yo^{u} deny?
Alleging *Caquirino*'s not at home
And yo^{u} haue vow'd perpetuall confinement
To yor chamber ~~if~~ vntill his safe returne?
Liset. Sure I should
Oret Why then you are an vndiscerning thing.
Dianora & my selfe are daylie visited
wth the most braue accomplish't gentlemen
The town affords, & if it chance that one
Of vs be not wthin the other straight
Giues a ready pleasing answer wch makes them still
Attend vs wth their frequent visitation,
When if we were like yo^{u}, they'd pass the dore
And cry, there dwell two pretty handsome women
But they want breeding, & it is a great pitty
× A well shap'd horse should want an easie pace.
Dia: 'Twas once my fortune to heare *Pagamino*
Mourn for yor ill fall'n lott because yo^{u} might not
Goe abroad as others doe.

[FOL. 203v/8v]

Liset Who *Pagamino*?
Dian. The same.
Liset. And he's a man of iudgement.
Dia. Incomparably wise
Oretta & my selfe when gallants come
× Take o^{r} right turnes, as watermen doe crie
I'm yor next man S^{r}

524 *is*] smeared for deletion

Liset. Are yo^{u} so open hearted?
Oret. 'Tis a great vertue to be counted hospitable
Liset. But not to all that come.
× *Dia.* Neuer to any that we think will tell.
Liset. I hate yor language & yor actions worse
And will not suffer my much iniur'd patience
To heare yo^{u} one word more. *One knocks.*
Who's there? Come in. *Enter Rinaldo.*
Rinald. Friar *Albert* & his copesmate *Ricciardo*
The holy brothers of *St Francis* order
Are come & say that this day is appointed
For the religious exercise of shrift
Liset. They're wellcome, 'pray inquire their sacred plesure
Whether I shall attend them where they are
Or they will take the paines to come in hither.
Rin: Ile p^{r}sently demand & then informe yo^{u}. *Exit.*
Liset. Will yo^{u} two be confest?
Dia. What say'st *Oretta*?
Oret. Yes if they will admitt vs thou & I
× Can tell a good deale more then we did last time.
Enter Rinaldo.
Rin: The holy men will enter p^{r}sently.
Liset. 'Tis well attend wthout. *Exit Rinaldo.*
Pray tell me one thing,
What is the meaning of a veniall sin?
Oret. Doe yo^{u} not vnderstand the cheefest tenent?
Any thing the preist will giue you leaue to doe,
by his permission yo^{u} may take a turn aboue
ground, & beat the Italian coruet & cõmitt
no offence.
Liset What doe yo^{u} meane by this?
× *Oret.* The explication of the riddle is, yo^{u} may cuckold
Yo^{r} husband & merit by it, so it be by the instigation
Of an holy broth^{r}. *Enter Albert & Ricciardo wth bell booke & Candle.*

9. [FOL. 204r]

Alb. Bless yo^{u} daughters, are yo^{u} well p^{r}par'd
To solemnize this cōmendable right?
Liset I am & these two if yo^{u} will admitt them. *She Cursies.*

Alb: Men of o^{r} function must not thrust back sinners
That wth repentant true acknowledgement
Of all their misdone acts mildly submitt
To all the questions & designed penance
We ask & please t'impose.
Di: & Oretta = We thank yor fauo^{r}
And will from hence remaine obedient daughters.
Alb: Be ready then, & as I doe cõmand
Or giue direction by my supreme beck
Submissiuely & willingly obey.
Ring out the holy bell, wch sacred sound
May lay the furies whose strange working power
Is p^{r}ualent where holines comes not.
Ricciardo rings the Bell.
the bell ceasing.
Alb: 'T hath bene a custome, & 'tis laudable
for many reasons not now to be discust
That all the auricular confession
W^{ch} any makes to vs, we must conceale
And take the inside of a penitent mind
No way but through this hole, *points to the hole in ye confessing chaire*
Lisetta come,
And wth a sin acknowledging deuotion *then sits in it.*
Explain yor guilty mind. *Lisetta makes cursie, comes to ye hole & seemes to speak, & Albert to answer her.*
Lisetta yo^{u}
Haue a most compendious way, & ether are
Less sinfull then oth^{r} women, or els yo^{u} haue
A very weak & small reteining memorie.
Liset. Pray please to giue me absolution S^{r}.
Alb: Content yor hasty mind vntill the rest
Haue eas'd their heauy consciences, & then
Ile wth a most paternall benediction
make yo^{u} all happy, *Dianora* & *Oretta*
As it falls out in yor vicissitude
Come neare & make confession, of each one side, one.
One of the one side of the Chaire, & the other on the other doe as Lisetta did, & the Friar Likewise.
O how yo^{u} ioy my heart wth this free plainenes.

[Fol. 204v/9v]

These sins yo^{u} speake of were done long agoe.
Oret. Not lately S^{r}.
Alb: How long may it be since?
Dia: Three dayes at least
Alb: Is this not lately?
Oret. I feel't no more then if't had not bene done
Therefore me thinks 'tis long agoe.
Alb: I chide yo^{u} wth my rod, & yor correction
Must be a strict obserued penance, by w^{ch}
In a priuate way Ile giue yo^{u} both direction
How yo^{u} shall expiate yor foule offence
And vnles willfullnes doe ou^{r}rule
The course of both yor liues yo^{u} may recouer
Yo^{r} selues out of great danger you may stand by.
Albert pawseth, then walks, speakes.
It is allowed for the good instruction
Of those that know not how to doe this duty
Completly as they ought, for vs to aske
A question though not at iust time of confession
Yet a little after, cheefely if it appeare
The party did not wth a setled grauitie
performe this needfull duty. Tell me *Lisetta*,
Haue yo^{u} not some paramour or seruant
The thought of whom when yo^{u} should haue bene ^ \serious/
made yor actions so fantastick?.
Liset. Yo^{u} ask a question
Deserues not to be answered, I haue a tie
forbids all such base loosenes my absent husband
To whom if I were not ingag'd, yo^{u} might
Haue leaue to descant on my beautie, but
No mortall be grac'd wth it's full fruition.
And if yo^{u} did but vnderstand so much
As yo^{u} profess yo^{u} doe, yor own discretion
Sufficientlie would tell yo^{u}, natures selfe
Kept holiday when she did make *Lisetta*,
And this well framed iewell no man aliue
Is worthy of but absent *Caquirino*.

641 *rod*] *d* altered   650 *not*] *n* written over *h*

Alb: Yo^{u} are a peece of lightnes & ou^{r}prize
The meane complexion yo^{u} are M^{ris} of.
Liset. Oh how yo^{u} stirr my blood, this 'tis to be
Subiect to bald pate slaues.

10. [FOL.205r]

Alb. You'l not reuile yor ghostly father?
Liset. But yet Ile boldly tell yo^{u}
Wherein yor iudgem^{t} errs, & while yo^{u} doe
Inioyne a thing wch is to be obeyed
Ile follow yor direction, but if yo^{u} dare
Oppose the open truth & discom̃end
My well composed feature, by yor leaue
Ile kick yor wise traditions, & nere be subiect
To him that manifestly doth me wrong.
Alb: Ile leaue yo^{u} to yor wise companions. *Ex. Alb: & Ricc:*
Liset. Graue S^{r} ~~faire~~
faire weather after yo^{u}, the blockish foole
Discerns not gold from copper.
Oret. Pox on't, this 'tis to spend yor time at home, do
yo^{u} think he durst haue vrg'd my patience so, that
trade abroad, & freely haue the company of all,
allthough he said I must doe penance, & that
he would inflict the same in priuate, yet he
× thought 'twas safer to leaue my blood vnchaf'd,
for womens spirits, like deuills once raisd will
hardly down againe .
Liset. Were't not for feare of getting an ill habit
I'd learne to scold against this ill=bred frier
Is not ill=bred a good word?
Orett. A most significant word for this occasion
Liset. Ile say what I was saying ouer againe, & then if
the words doe not stand right find fault, & tell
me how they may be better placed.
Oret. Ile rep^{r}hend if there be cause.
Liset. Rep^{r}hend? that's a good word too.
Oret. O that is a prime word if a woman vse it
to her husband.
Liset Well but as I said,

685 ~~*faire*~~] smeared for deletion 696 *Were't*]*'t* inserted

Were it not for feare of getting an ill habit
I'd learn to scold against this ill=bred frier
should come againe.
Oret. Beleeu't, 'tis no ill habit sometimes for breuitie
to nickname yor husband, & call him *Will*, or *Tom*,
onely to practise yor tong, that when yor patience
is prouok't, yo^{u} may reward him that abuseth yo^{u}.
Liset. Yet me thinks such terms as these were bett^{r} vented

[Fol. 205v/10v]

Vpon the kitchin boy or any man
Of meaner ranck, then on a womans husband.
Oret. I'd call him foole to choose, for if it chance
His blood be chaf'd, & he thereon take pett
In time 'twill down againe & he impute
It onely to the purenes of yor mettle.
Dia. Or els yo^{u} may doe this & heale the wound
Yo^{r} fault, but think't not so, hath made, come to him
Kiss him & say, why, doest thou think fond man
I doe not loue thee most extremely Sirrah?
And take it of my honest word *Lisetta*,
If any deuill be vp this trick will lay him.
Liset. It may be not, & what's to be. done then?
Dia: Leaue him at home, & slight him & become
Acquainted wth a gentleman oth' horse
To some great man, & by this meanes yo^{u} may
At yor own plesure whirle along the streets
In his Lords coach, wch royall priuiledge
Will fill yor mind wth farr more lofty thoughts
Then thinking of a husband in the country
Or gone from home.
Oret. Well thought on *Dianora*, they're both good wayes.
Liset. And if I haue occasion, Ile see what fruit yor
councell will bring forth.
+ *Dia*: I am glad to see yor vnderstanding edified.
Liset. No vndertaking's rais'd to eminence
But hath the helpe of time, nor can a day
Send forth a ꝑfect scholler, & if I doe
Reape any vsefull profitt by th'aduise

728 *be.*] stop possibly accidental ink spot

I haue receau'd from yo^{u}, Ile not acknowledge
My selfe a more well wisher to my selfe
Then my obseruant actions shall declare
Me yor ingaged freind for euery woman
Hath cause to value those her dearest freinds
That set her in a way to work her ends. *Ex: Ões.*

Fin: Act. 2.

Act. 3. Enter Bergamino, Landolpho, Rinaldo. [Act 3, scene i]

Rin: I know tis ill to sow dissentious seed
'Twixt those that are allied, or feigne a cause

11. [Fol. 206r]

from whence might grow a troublous discontent
Among vnited friends.
Berg: Are those the women
Yo^{u} say that keep her company?
Rin: The same, doe yo^{u} think Ile tell yo^{u} an vntruth.
Land: Vsed they to come, & visit her before yor m^{r} went?
Rin: Once, & no more, but he did much mislike it
And strictly charg'd me, that if I did perceaue
They frequently did visit her, I should make known
The same to yo^{u}, wch I doe faithfully.
Berg: Why these two are the veriest twekes in *Venice*. |
Land: The more to be auoided.
Rin: You hitt it right S^{r}, & the only lecture
They read to her as I am well informd
By one that will not lye.
Berg: Who's that?
Rin: Obedience; is how a woman may wth skill & ease
Ore reach her husband, & make him a meere gregory.
Lan: A gregory what's that?
Rin: An elder brother, or if youl hau't in English
A down right foole S^{r}.
These lasses haue a queint compos'd receipt
By wch direction they can make a medicine,
And yet th'ingedients are but ordinary,
W^{ch} if a woman rightly doe apply
Vnto her husbands forehead, the skin will grow
Forthwth so pure & thin, that sodainly

Not this

745 *receau'd*] *au* altered and blotted

Strange things call'd horns will sprout vpon his ‸ \brow/,
Yet he shall nere ꝑceaue it, nay wch is more
They'l teach a woman that will apply her mind
To learn to doe the trick at one time dressing.
Ber: Did *Obedience* giue yo^{u} this light.
Rin: No S^{r},
This generall receipt they doe diuulge
As Mountebanks proclaime their oyles & balsam
On open stages, but if you please Ile call her
And make no question but she will inform yo^{u}
Of that youl wonder at.
Berg. Pray goe & call her *Ex: Rinaldo.*

[Fol. 206v/11v]

'Tis a well meaning fellow, or *Caquirino*
Would not relye so confidently on him
As put his whole estate into his hands
We therefore must beleeue his information
Vntill we heare a reason contrary.
Lan: Contein yor selfe reseruedly, vntill
You haue some further notice, ꝑhaps this wench
Had some strange dreame last night, & she to vent it
Hath said *Dianora* or *Oretta* coyn'd it. *Enter Rin: & Obedience.*
Ber: *Obedience* yo^{u} must make a true relation
Of all the passages that were between
Yo^{r} m^{ris} *Dianora* & *Oretta*
When they were last together.
Ob: There were no passages at all among them, for
while they were together, they onely did sitt
still & talk.
Ber: Thou thinkst, thou hast a share of witt,
but tis a meane one, what did they talk of
when they were together?
Ob: Of things, & things, & many pretty things
such as pleas'd them.
Ber: Tell me what were those things?
Ob: My m^{ris} taught them to flourish network, &
they told her how she might play at fast & loose.
Lan: O vile wench
Ob: Why there's no hurt in't, what harme doth

a woman pray, when she playes at fast & loose
wth a string. *Rinaldo* lend me yor garter, come
+ be not ashamed to vntie, Ile doe no hurt wth't,
looke you thus,   *she doth a trick of fast &*
fast or loose for a   *loose wth his garter.*
row of pins, now 'tis fast, & now 'tis loose, 'tis
an easie trick, yet cannot be learn'd wthout
teaching, & thus they droue away the tedious
howres.

Lan: And gaue iust cause to all licentious tongs
To call their names in question; those daies were /blest\

12 [Fol. 207r]

When women nere saw man, beside their fathers
Till they were one & thirty, & if a woman
Wth a reserued modestie exceeding
The expectation, wch the world had on her,
Did chance at nine & twenty to be maried,
She euery day would for a yeare or two
Blush in her modest vaile, being much asham'd
'Twas her hard chance to know a man so ~~y<ounge>~~ ^ \soone../

Ob: Those were the dayes of ignorance when women
Knew not their own abilitie, nor how
To value their own worth, when old men vs'd
To name their daughters patience inferring
They must eat no nuts till they drop't of the trees
And haue no husbands till their fathers pleasd.

Not this

Lan: And therein shew'd the vnexampled duty
Those happy times were blest wth.

Ob: Nay therein shew'd
The scuruy, paltry, seruile, slauish awe
W^{ch} water spaniells shew to falconers.
for if a braue spirited wench had but intreated
The company of a man (whose handsomenes
And other things could not at all be faulted)
And the old doting foole had but mislik'd it,
(for that's the name yong wenches giue their fath^{r}ꝛ)

Not this

820 *pray*] ink mark after *y*; could be a flourish or the start of an incomplete *?*   830 *blest*] added below line, preceded by a rounded L bracket   838 ~~*y<ounge>*~~ ^ *\soone../*] ~~*y<ounge>*~~ smeared for deletion; caret below ~~<ou>~~ of ~~*y<ounge>*~~

She must haue wth a crouching low obedience
Renounc'd the quarry, as if a setting dog
Had heard his tirannous master cry, 'ware that.
Ber: Sure she has bene a falconers wife.
Ob: No but I haue bene exercisd in stiching Iesses.
Ber: Very good; & since yo^{u} know other womens be=
hauiour to ward their fathers, so well, pray
what's yor own, when yor father is in place?
Ob: My father?
Ber: Yo^{r} father I say, yo^{u} had one had yo^{u} not?
Ob: Yes.
Ber: Of what nation?
Ob: My mother was an English woman.
Rin: Yo^{r} father Signieur *Bergamino* asks for.

[Fol. 207v/12v]

Ob: And I can tell him who my mother was, but not
my father.
Rin: How so *Obedience*?
Ob: Yo^{r} question's quickly answer'd, for in England
The m^{ris} sometimes loues her man farr better
Then she doth her husband, & then the fellow sweats ^ \for't/
Sometimes a Courtlike gallant comes in brisk
And offering her his seruice ꝑhaps cõmitts,
And though one of these two get the child,
What matter is't, so the husband haue the credit?
Now for me to vndertake who my father was, before
I was borne or thought of, in respect of the acci=
dents fore=spoken, & perhaps foredone, I must desire
Yo^{r} pardon & my fathers, whosoeuer he be, onely
this I will say, my mother was an English woman,
& reasonable handsome, she was a tollerable pro=
uocation, & a sufficient remediũ.
Rin. What, Latin?
Ob: I learn't it of a scholler came lately from the
vniu^{r}sitie, who hath a booke that proues a
woman to be a remedium.

857 *'ware*] apostrophe written low and then repeated in correct position 860 *Very good;*] upper dot of semi-colon unclear 861 *to ward*] = *toward*

Rin: Gentlemen will yo^{u} giue me leaue to thrust one question to her.

Ber: Yes

Rin: Since yo^{u} know not who was yor father, I pray tell me who was yor godfather?

Ob: Why doe yo^{u} ask?

Rin: Because of the strangenes of yor name.

Ob: My godfather neuer had to doe wth naming me *Obedience*, but foure or fiue vnhappy pages the other day went about an exercise they call'd swearing of pages, & this was to be done in a roome in a tauern next o^{r} washhouse, wher gilian & I were smoothing linnen, & we two enuying the rascalls happines, for we saw them through a chink drinking like lords, concluded, we would haue a day of swearing chambermaids, & so we had, at wch time I was named *Obedience*, & com̃anded

13 [Fol. 208r]

that if any man ask'd why I was so called I should answer in a verse, wch he that taught me had a strange name for.

Rin. What a Saphick verse?

Ob. No it did not rime.

Rin. Pentameter?

Ob: A meter is a kin to't.

Rin. Oh then tis Hexameter.

Ob: Iust; but he bade me, I should tell those that question'd me about my name, that there is a verse for't, & that is this, *she scans it, Like a latin (verse*

My name is not natiue but by worthy desert got,

& that there was authority for my name, and authority is not to be spoken against except it be in a drunken constable or a foolish Iustice of peace.

Rin. Who taught yo^{u} this?

Ob: The gentleman scholler that taught me the word.

Rin. The word, what word?

Ob: + The word that is Latin for a woman, *remedium*.

897 *naming*] *a* altered, possibly from *e* 901 *washhouse*] ²*h* written over *b*

Ber: And by what worthy desert did yo^{u} get yor name?
Ob: We were shewing tricks, & gilian was appointed
to lay her heele in her neck, wch she did most finely,
& thereupon the Lady of misrule called her nimble,
& asked me that suppose another <..>man were
in bed wth my m^{ris}, & my m^{r} should knock, if my m^{ris}
bade me hold the dore I could not doe it, while
the man yo^{u} wote of slipt into the closet, I said:
Yes, stept to the dore & cried, & thereupon she calld
me *Obedience*, & since that time I haue bene euer
great wench or little woman *Obedience*.
Ber: <.> Well *Obedience*, since yor name is *Obedience*, I am
sory, yo^{u} take no more care to be obseruant, & obedient
to the lawes of vertue & chastitie.
Ob. We are sworn to the contrary, & it is part of the
+ chambermaids oath, neuer to think chast thought
till the mark be out of her mouth, & for deeds,
when we cannot bring o^{r} resolution to action &
execution, we must be quiet, sit down wth loss &
think the more:
Ber: I must intreat yo^{u} that allthough yor mind

[Fol. 208v/13v]

Be wantonly addicted, to forbeare
To vtter light & vnbeseeming words
Before yor m^{ris}
Ob: My master's not at home
And he being absent my m^{ris} is my M^{r}
Vntill he come againe, & by a habit wch she if she
be wise may get by practise, she'l come so in the
fashion, that her will when he comes back againe
will beare such sway, that he shall crouch to her
& not oppose what ere her plesure is in confi=
dence of w^{ch} & hope she'l doe her selfe this right,
if she please to inioyne me to conteine my thoughtꝭ
which often work for her aduantage, Ile barr my
selfe the womans priuiledge, the motion of my
× tong, & like a bride simper & say iust nothing, but
Yo^{r} com̃and & vnregarded words shall not debarr

931 <..>*man*] deletion smeared 938 <.>] blotted 941] SP high

me of my greatest plesure the vse of talking.
Ber: Thou art a hopeles thing & may'st be likened
to a whelp that runs at sheep, wch courteous words
cannot reclaime, but sharp correcting blowes, will
make him clapp his taile between his legs lye
down & whine, *Rinaldo* weel goe in, & take aduise
how this fast growing euill may be p^{r}uented.
Rin: Ile attend yo^{u} S^{r}. *Ex: Ber: Lan: Rinaldo*
Ob: You're three sweet begles, iust a knott of fooles;
If thou wer't not my Mistres elder brother
Id make these nailes ingraue it i'thy face
I scorn thy base comparison, but want of witt
makes thee doe this, & it is no wonder
Thou hast so little vnderstanding, since
Thou wearest thy haire vnpoudered.
Lis: wthin. Obedience, Obedience I say.
Ob: Yo^{r} plesure forsooth
Lis: wthin. Come quickly starch my gorget & my band.
Of the new fashion, those both of one lace
for i th' afternoone I meane to goe abroad
And weare my beuer hat
Ob: I doubt there's no starch made. *Exit Ob:*
Enter at the other dore, Albert & Ricciardo. [Act 3, scene ii]
Alb. The priuiledge is vnvaluable, that lay people
Wth a deuout mind giuing all they haue

14. [FOL. 209r]

To o^{r} societie, may reape the benefit
Of being slightly punishd in purgatory.
Ricc. The ignorant haue no way els to meritt.
But yet my conscience makes a kind of doubt
Whether't be lawfull to perswade a man
To giue vs all he hath, & let his wife
And children goe a begging.
Alb. Yo^{u} wrong o^{r} order
Inmaking such a doubt, what if St Francis
Call'd pouertie a Lady, yet wee're not bound
To follow his example & adore
An Idoll, that giues nether meat nor clothes,

972 *You're*] start of superscript *u* after *o* 987 *that*] written over *w^{ch}* 997 *Inmaking*] *n* inserted

If he be in a good mind lay closely to him
Tell him he's damn'd vnles he giue vs all
And then thou art a braue proficient.
Ricc. I, but my conscience & the wife & children
Cannot be then at peace.
Alb. What, conscience sayst thou?
There's no more conscience to be made of getting
A lay mans estate then for a lawyer to take fees;
'Tis but a fee, & if he giue it not
Weel not giue leaue that he shall goe to heauen.
But tell him no mony, no heauen, & if thou be
So scuruily hen hearted, that thy pitty
Will needs defraud vs of o^{r} proper goods,
Because forsooth the brats must be maintain'd
And the wife not begg, giue the widow when /she is one\
A cow to giue her milk & euery child
A peny a weeke to set it forth to schoole.
Ricc: But will this serue?
Alb. If it will not let it choose.
Ricc. Gold is a powerfull charme, & will ~~quiet~~ \charme/
☞ × The hardest bitten dog ith' world, a Vsurer.
farewell *Albert* what success I haue
Ile giue thee iust account of. *Exit*
Alb. Mony enough & all is well enough.
Now for my busines *Albert knocks.*
Ob: wthin. What sawcy knaue is that?
Alb. It is frier *Albert.* *Enter Ob: & kneeles*
Ob: Forgiue me holy father that my hast
Made ‸\mee/ forget my duty.

[Fol. 209v/14v]

She kneeles

Alb Kiss my toe, & this great sin's forgiu'n. *She kisseth his toe.*
And henceforth euer let yor wary tong
Vtter no words but in adoration
Of o^{r} religious brotherhood.

1005 *Cannot*] *C* altered from *T* 1015 */she is one*] insertion below line, preceded by a square L bracket to separate it from the text in l. 1016. 1020 *~~quiet~~*] underlined for deletion and *charme* interlined above in lighter ink 1030 *She kneeles*] *knee* smeared; SD high; possibly added later

Ob. I will be carefull |*riseth*
Alb. Is yor m^{ris} faire *Lisetta* wthin?
Ob: She's in her chamber.
Alb. Tell her I intreat
She'l please to afford me but the courteous fauour
I may speake a word or two in priuate wth her.
Ob. Ile let her know yor mind. *Exit.*
Alb. 'Tis a braue thing
That I that was but *Bertho de la massa*
A base reputed cheat in *Imola*
Should vndertaking a religious order
Be held in such esteeme, that all the citty
Doe bow their seruile heads in adoration
Of me their holy father; power vsurp't
Still keepes the ignorant in greatest awe
And that wch gaines me honour & cōmoditie
I'm sure tis good to practise; *Albert* goe on,
This is a way to get thee gold & plesure.
My plot=contriuing thoughts might haue deni'd
My body strength repairing sleep, & I
Haue got a small reward of troublous cares
Had I liu'd still in *Imola*. For euery man
Did so much slight my lye=relating tales
And what my tong reported, that I could scarce
Get credit to procure me meat & lodging.
But the holines professing name of Frier
Strikes terrour in the simple, & makes them open
Their close lockt hords to offer at my shrine;
It makes the wealth ingrossing vsurer
In hope to ease his soule of paine to constitute
Me soly his executour, & if it chance
I eat some lust prouoking delicates
That stirr my body wth an vnusuall heat
I get me to the handsomst wife of those
That destine me their heire, & there vnload
Me of my troublous burden; this way I doe
Cōmand the mens soules, & the womens bodies
And find religion vsefull. */Enter Lisetta & Obedience.*

Lis: 'Tis a wonder
That yo^{u} whose strength of will, yet not of iudgem^{t}
Praiseth yor merit, should make so low descent
As yeeld a freindly seeming visitation
To me that am so despicable.
Alb: Errour reform'd
Makes cleare ey'd truth the more conspicuous,
And a delinquent that acknowledgeth
His fault & begs forgiuenes meriteth
A signed pardon, please yo^{u} cõmand
Yo^{r} maid to leaue the roome, & Ile impart
The reason of this admirable change
And shew ^ \you/ greater secrets.
Lis: Goe in Obedience. *Exit Ob*:
Alb. He that is blinded, wth the foggy mists
Of ignorance, discerns not good from euill,
Vntill it please some strong inlightned power
To driue away the truth obscuring vapours
And make a cleare way for his vnderstanding.
My curse was to be blind; & my iust doome
Would haue remain'd an euerlasting punishment
To me & my posteritie, had not a power
Greater then mortall bene compassionate
And taken pitty of my penitent greefe.
For the last night, when heauy sleep began
": To close my weary lids, I hear'd a noise
Equall to that the euen=poysed earth
Makes when it mouing trembles, & no sooner
were mine eares filled wth this hideous sound
But I began to suffer, & vndergoe
An easeles torment, the reason was alleg'd
And whisper'd in mine eare, by whom I know not
'Twas for neglecting yo^{u}, whereat I cried
Ease me, for I repent; 'Twould not be granted
Vntill I bound my selfe by sacred oath
To craue yor now petitioned forgiuenes

1074 *strength*] *gt* altered 1076 *yeeld*] *y* possibly written over another character or altered
1085 *shew* ^ *\you/ greater*] caret below *g* of *greater*; *you* interlined in darker ink 1088 *euill*] *i* blotted
1100 *sooner*] blotted above *r*

Lis: Who was't I pray that gaue yo^{u} this due punishm^{t}?
Alb. 'Tis death to tell you, till you grant me pardon,
But when yor gracious mercy shall vouchafe
To say I am forgiuen, I must relate
Things wch the weake capacitie of mortalls
When they are told will think incredible;
Yet I must let yo^{u} know, & you'l perceaue,
They are not fictions, but truths reall essence.

[FOL. 210V/15V]

Lis. May I beleeue yo^{u}?
Alb. All the protestations
That tongs of men can make, I will repeat,
And if you will not suffer yor beleefe
To credit these, doe but appoint the thing
You'l haue me call to witnes & I will sweare by't.
Lis: I will not haue yo^{u} sweare, yet I forgiue you.
Alb. God *Cupid* giue you thanks for't, who p^{r}sents
His seruice to yo^{u}, & is so enamour'd
Of yor celestiall beauty, that he thinks
(*Venus* exepted) heauen nor earth containes
A beautie whose illustrious eminence
Can check yo^{u} wth compare.
Lis: Doe yo^{u} abuse me?
Alb. No otherwise then I wish to wrong my soule.
For the amorous god the last night did appeare
Cloth'd as he's pictur'd, & gaue castigation
To me for my delinquencie, & had not
His mercy & my penitence bene obuious
I had suffer'd death, because my ill rul'd tong
Disparaged yor beauties excellence
wth vnregardles words
Lis. O how a god
Exceeds you friers in knowledge,! th'vnknowing he‸\a/rdman
So priz'd *Europa*, when the transformed god
Vouchaf'd to carry her on his able back
And gloried in his burden.
Alb. I cannot speake

1138 *vnregardles*] *les* altered from *ed*   1140 *!*] inserted   1141 *god*] *d* altered from *e*

But I shall erre, therefore I implore
Yo^{r} mercy wth my silence, & those words
× W^{ch} my repentant tong is bound to vtter
To giue yo^{u} satisfaction, I will repeat
And so oft cause my humble knee to make
A lowly flexure, as I ought to speake. *Conge's oft*:
Lis. It is enough, but is the god in loue?
Alb. Wth yo^{u} extremely, & he hath so ingag'd
Himselfe to doe yo^{u} seruice that he hath oft
Pleasd ~~yor~~‸ \him<.>/=selfe wth yor plesure yeelding face
And lean'd vpon yor pillow, while yo^{u} slept
Onely to view the rarities, wch he
Tooke comfort in beholding, & would haue wak'd
not trans= cribed Yo^{u} that he might haue seen the full perfection
W^{ch} enuious sleep debarr'd him of but that
He fear'd so sodaine a disturbance might

16. [Fol. 211r]

Giue yo^{u} some cause of feare.
Lis. The god is wise
And where so ere I see his glorious picture
Ile reare a burning taper.
Alb. That wch is more,
He bad me tell you that to manifest
The truth of his affection doe but set downe
What shape yo^{u} please he shall come to yo^{u} in
And what time you desire to see his brightnes
And if he ether miss the time or shape
Think him no god but mortall
Lis: 'Twere p^{r}sumption
To offer to confine a god in limitts.
Alb. Yet for yor sake because he is a spirit
And so no humane eye can looke vpon
Him as he is himselfe, nor wthout dazleing
The optick sense, behold the radiant lustre
His glory doth eiect, he'l be yor seruant
In what shape best contents yo^{u}, be it yor husbands

1152 *extremely*] *m* altered 1154 ~~yor~~‸ \him<.>/=selfe] caret partly overwritten by apostrophe in *lean'd* in l. 1155; <.> possibly a character written over superscript *r* of ~~yor~~ and then deleted; = inserted 1174] SP high

Or any other mans.

Lis: My husbands? no,
I once in errour thought the world afforded
No comfort like my husbands company,
☞ But now I thank my starrs & wholesome councell
I am reform'd, therefore let the god
Appeare as he best pleaseth, & Ile receaue
Him wth a gratefull wellcome,ꝓuided allwayes
He doe renounce all the obligations
He's ti'd to other women in & bend
His able strength, & youthfull actiuenes
To work my sole content.

Alb. My memory
Fail'd in that point, but not the gods respect.
Honour'd *Lisetta*, if it may not iniure
Yor worth, wch now doth stand in more esteeme
wth me then this sweet aire, wch breath maintaines
my life as fire prserues heat, Ile be bold
To make one poore request, wch if you grant
You'l shew yor nature kind & mercifull
To one that meritts little, & those that are
Good to the vndeseruing, get more praise
Then they ‸\yt/ doe vouchafe a fauour to
Their seruants that haue toyl'd for't, my offence

[Fol. 211v/16v]

Call's for contempt from you, & if yor goodnes
In stead of blaming raise my low brought soule
wth sorrow to one step of happines
You'l gain a great renown, & when you die
Haue tropheies rais'd to grace yor memorie:
My suite hath hitherto bene so obscure
for feare you should not grant it, but my boldnes
Hath now got heart & humbly doth intreat
You'l daign the god's appearance may be to you
In my peculiar bodily shape & then
You may wthout taxation of the world
Or satisfying curious inquisition

1196 *me*] *m* written over start of *t* 1197 *my*] curved pen stroke above *m* 1205 *In stead*] = *Instead*
1209 *suite*] *i* inserted

Reape yor desir'd delights, & frier *Albert*
Yo^{r} to yor mercy most obliged seruant
Inioy a heauenly bliss, for while the god
On earth assumes my shape & vseth it,
my not to be imagin'd happines
will be in heauen, & my ioyfull soule
Wander in louers paradise, & feele
The sweetnes of their vnexprest felicitie.

Liset. 'Tis a request wch reason must giue eare to
And I will grant, since this small courtesie
Can no way make the least part of requiteall
Because you vnderwent so sore a punishment
When the god first chastis'd yo^{u}.

Alb. Thankfull praise
I yeeld you from a most obseruant heart,
And giue you one note more, the god assuming
A humane shape will enter at the dore
And there you wth obedient submission
Must entertain him in humilitie
And offer odours wth a holy mind.

Lis. Ile haue all done to th' purpose, take no care
And think I'm *Venus* for the god of warr. *Ex: Ambo.*

Fin. Act. 3.

Act. 4. *Enter Rinaldo, & Obedience.* [Act 4, scene i]

Rin. Prethee Obedience ‸\neuer stand vpon't/, it is a thing nature's prone to, & therefore let vs *Concubere.*

Ob: How if I should proue wth child?

Rin. That's a hundred to one, but if thou fearest it, the mountebank that shewes tricks vpon the *Rialto* will vndertake to p^{r}uent it for halfe a crown, & that Ile pay.

not transcribed

17. [Fol. 212r]

Ob. I doe not like to haue any dealing wth him, because he thrusts his ‸\man/ through wth a dagger & that

Rin: Then thou shalt haue a Court phisician ‸,\ for they are tender fingred rascalls/ ~~for they~~ &
cause abortions as often, as they giue the wai=

1242] SP high   1248 *phisician* ‸,\ *for … rascalls*/] caret below *n* of *phisician*

not this | ting women aloes, & make no more bones on't,
then a wench that has the green sicknes do's
to take steele losinges.

Ob. But to take phisick in this case may bring dan=
ger to my body.

Rin. Then goe to't the down right way, & if thou
perceaue an alteration in thy body, (as I heard
a gentlewoman say that had bene but two
dayes maried) then p^{r}sently lay't vpon the schoole=
master, & this fooles back is broad enough to
carry a greater burden.

Ob. But grant all this were done, how should we liue?

Rin. Ile giue him an *Vrsin's* catachisme, & a *Beza's* tes=
tament, for few country <.......> *Domine's* vse
more bookes, & wth the help of these he may learn
to preach, & by preaching often, & flattering a
country gentleman, he may perhaps get a liuing
Θ of twenty pound a yeare that is in his gift.

Ob: This will not serue to buy him clokes wth veluet
capes, & doe you think I will not weare wosted
stockings.

Rin: Then to mend his reuenue he may make wills, &
by ꝑswading the testator to be in a good mind, & for
his paines in writing, he'l get at least ten shilings,
but if it be a healthfull parish, & those few that
Die, haue not so much to dispose of, as the writing
of a will comes to, he may trade in making bonds
for a groat a peece, & drawing indentures for
halfe a crown a paire.

Ob. All this while you talk how he shall get, but what
shall I doe, make shirts for six pence a peece, & cuffs
For two pence a paire.

Rin. | Farr be it from me so to wrong thy sweetnes
my louing care shall make so great prouision

[Fol. 212v/17v]

Thou shalt want nothing. Ile bring thee beuer hats,
Imbroidered gloues, & kniues wth golden strings,

1251 *do's*] *s* written over smeared character, possibly *y*   1271] SP high

Eare wires of siluer, & a scarlet peticoat,
And ‸\if/ I find thou giu'st me daintie content,
I will not stick wth thee for a ‸\white/ shag wascot
Or two to weare in sum̃er.
Ob: The thred shag & the beuer hat, me thinks
doe not agree
Rin. They shall be sattin then or damask wch thou wilt.
Ob: I care not which, but I would faine haue that
costs most, for parsons wiues goe finer now then
Ladies in old time.
Rin. They shall be of the dearest stuff that can be gott,
but the very quintessence of the busines is yet
Vnspoke of, wch is where & when?.
Ob: You say, true, & the very marow bone of the matt^{r}
(as m^{r} *Rombus* said) is left vnpickt, vnles there
be another thing done, which is, you must part
wth some gold, & earnest the bargaine, for they say
gold binds, & no bargain 's good especially in these
cases wthout a golden earnest.
Rin. What shall I pay the keeper a fee before my
warrant be seru'd.
Ob. If yo^{u} doe not, yo^{u} must giue his wife some
feeling afore hand, & the flesh will proue the better.
Rin. Thou art for me on all sides, here *giues her gold.*
Ob: This pill will work to th' purpose, & if I be not
As soly at thy seruice as the mattres
Is at the fetherbeds wch lies vnder it,
Neuer call me more Obedience
But a downright Chambermaid. *Exitura.*
Rin. Nay stay, the time & place?
Ob: Yet again, Ile tell thee in thine eare *whisps.*
Rin. Well but suppose ———————— *he whisps.*
Ob: What? ————————
Rin: That. ————————
Ob. Paw waw dost not vnderstand?
Rin: ‸\O there there/ Well 'tis enough farewell. *Exiturus*

1287 *if*/] interlined in darker ink 1292 *wilt*] *t* altered from *l* 1321 ‸*O there there*/] caret below *t* of '*there*

Ob: Now stay yo^{u} S^{r}, haue yo^{u} no more to doe?

18. [Fol. 213r]

Rin. No not till then.

Ob: What? blab? why yo^{u} dull foole, did yo^{u} euer see
a seruant leaue his m^{ris} wthout a parting kiss?

Rin. In truth I had forgot.

Ob: And you'l forgiue me if I forget?

Rin: Oh talk not of forgetting, I had busines in my head
made me slow.

Ob: And if it chance some busines in my head make me
forget to keep my word wth you, youl not be angry?

Rin. No more I prethee but kiss & be freinds.

Ob: Now I will not, downe vpon yor knees, desire me
to forgiue yo^{u}, then rise vp make me a leg, kiss
Yo^{r} hand & then kiss me. *he doth so & when he is about to kiss her she turns round about & stands wth her back to him.*

Rin: Art thou in earnest?

Ob: O yor coy chambermaid is as much
in fashion as yor painted lady, yet I
can lay my strangenes in a fitt time
as well as she doth her complexion ith' night,
& to make this good, come now Ile kiss thee. *Kisseth him*

Rin: farewell sweet heart prethee do not miss

Ob: Miss say you? *Ex. Rin.*
He that giues a wench gold, & forgetts to kiss her,
When he thinks he shall haue her, shall be sure to miss ^\her./. *Ex Ob:*

Enter Lisetta, Dianora, & Oretta.

Dia: 'Tis the vnhappines of vs not to be able [Act 4, scene ii]
To requite yor many fauours, yet yo^{u} know
what vnderstanding yo^{u} haue gott by following
Th' aduise we dayly giue yo^{u}.

Lis: I acknowledge it,
And must confess my selfe not to deserue
So trusty councellours, nor know I how to pay
The debt I owe yo^{u}.

Dia. Yo^{u} are no whit engag'd
To vs, but when we saw yo^{u} liue in ignorance
We thought 'twas sin to leaue yo^{u} still in darknes;

1341 *this*] *i* altered 1351 *acknowledge*] *c* altered 1355 *Yo^{u}*] dash below *u*

And if it please yo^{u} to extend yor goodnes
So farr, as help o^{r} hard oppressing wants
wth a little sum̃ of mony, you will raise
Yo^{r} worth as high as heauen, & giue vs cause
To stile yo^{u} one of o^{r} prime benefacto^{r}c.

[Fol. 213v/18v]

Lis: I haue not much about me, but all I haue
Is yo^{r}c, I wish it more, but cannot stay. [*Giues them money, then* *Ex:*/
Dia. We humbly thank yo^{u}, & are eu^{r} yo^{r}c.
Oret. It is the misery of witt to be poore, & yet it is the
happines of it againe often to raise something out
of nothing, as now we haue
merchants imploy their facto^{r}c, Kings their agents,
And both are oft less vsefull then expensiue,
Yet haue their exhibition duly paid,
And why should not *Lisetta* who receaues
more good from vs then they from them be liberall?
Dia. It is a faire beginning, 'pray do not blame her
Till yo^{u} haue more cause.
Oret. I doe not blame her
not this ┼ But onely speake this to take of th'aspersions
wch fooles might cast vpon her for this freenes.
Dia. Yo^{u} know where yo^{u} haue promised to be
Therefore let's goe.
Oret. I, we two thou knowest must play at gleeke wth a
Yong gentleman, thou shalt sits on's hand, & I
will tread o' thy foot whensoeuer I haue Tib, & then
he shall buy the stock, & so weel cheat the gull.
Dia. A vsefull plot. *Exeunt Ambœ.*

Enter ^*at the other dore,*/ *Lisetta, & Obedience perfuming.*

Lis: Is that the perfume according to the Archduches [Act 4, scene iii]
receipt?
Ob: The very same.
Lis: Goe in, & stay ith' chamber till I call yo^{u}. *Ex. Ob*:

Lis: walks, Enter Alb: like Cupid she kneeles.

1382 *sits*] terminal *s* deleted by blotting 1385 *Ambœ*] *œ* written over *o*

Alb. Kneeling is call'd the suppliants humble posture
And therefore fit's not yo^{u}, rise beauteous m^{ris}.
And tast completely those delicious ioyes
Others are proud to heare of; *Kisseth her, she Cursies,*
Againe my loue *Kisseth againe, she cursies.*
Spare the obseruant bending of yor knees
And be bonere & buxome, gods that descend
To tast *Venetian* beauties, must be free,
Like those they come to, & giue libertie
As much as they can wish.
Lis: Will yo^{u} giue leaue

19. [Fol. 214r]

I may kiss yo^{u} when I will?
Alb. Yes & perswade
Yo^{r} selfe yo^{u} haue not so much priuiledge
Ouer a man on earth, as yor cleare fairenes
Hath giu'n yo^{u} power on *Cupid*, who forsooke
His place in heauen design'd, & did assume
A mortall shape, because his glorious brightnes
Would haue consum'd a terren feminine weakenes
wth the first apparition. But had I known
Yo^{r} not till now discern'd serenitie
Had so surpast the low=pris'd dignitie
Ladies vsurp in thought, & yet fall short of
my rarely woman gracing maiestie
And loue repelling, & inciteing power
Should haue appear'd wth all the complemen^{t}⊏
That fitt *Lisetta's* seruant, *Cupids* deitye.
Lis: Is any woman happy but my selfe?
Or doth my hearing or my seeing faile me?
Are yor words words, & so myne eares capacitie
Is able to app^{r}hend them? or the obiect
Mine eyes behold a fiction or realitie?
Alb. It is th' inherent property of loue
To striue to help, but neuer to deceaue;
And should it once be noys'd among the gods
That I were hipocriticall, Iustice her selfe
Displeasd would rend my quiuer from my back

not y^{is} And breake my twanging bow, prohibiting
Them euer future power. And as a herald
when he degrade's a worthles knight, pulls of
His sword & then his spurrs, & first breakes flatwayes
The thing that gaue him honour, then in contempt
Kicks his despised spurrs; so equall *Iustice*,
Found she me conscious of this hatefull crime,
Would from her to all right affording throne
Step down in furie & snatch of all my ornamentꞇ.
Men may deceaue, but gods are not erroneous.
Lis: I reuerence yor vndoubted truth, the messenger
Yo^{u} sent to warn me of yor sacred com̃ing
Bad I should ^\burne/ some choice compos'd perfume
When I thought yo^{u} would enter

[FOL. 214V/19V]

Alb. My Nostrills still
Sent ~~feele~~ yor obseruance to me, & me thinks
Tis like the incense fumes vpon ~~the~~ o^{r} altars.
Haue yo^{u} not in some inner roome a bed
On wch I might reuiue the wearied lim̃s
Of frier *Albert*? for I, no sooner left
The whirling spheres, but I assum'd his shape.
Lis. ____ There is a chamber drest but not in state
fitt for a god to come in;
Alb: I much desire
To see that roome, & by that strong allie
whereby my loue's inchained to yor merit. ,
Ingage yo^{r}selfe neuer to leaue me, while
I please to abide in that roome or on earth.
Lis: The happines my heart desir'd, but yet my fearefull tong
Durst not intreat, yor fauour granting goodnes
Daignes to afford, & makes yor in hart ~~petitioner~~
Petitioner haue the disposing power
Of granting her own wishes.
Alb: I came on earth
Onely to doe yo^{u} seruice, & if it please
Yo^{u} but to lead me in to that priuate place

1430] stop raised 1432 *flatwayes*] *e* written over *t* 1439] SP high 1444 *Sent*] added in darker ink in L margin 1448 ?] possibly inserted 1456 *abide*] *e* possibly added *that*] ²*t* altered, possibly from *r* 1459 ~~*petitioner*~~] inked out for deletion

wch yo^{u} haue nam'd, & I so long to be in,
Ile shew yo^{u} there the misteries of loue
Exceeding farr the misteries of state
(So rumored in the world) for depth & working.

Lis: This is the way, please yo^{u} goe in Ile follow. *Ex Amb.*

Enter Bergamino, Landolpho, & Rinaldo.

Ber: When did you receaue the letter, *Rinaldo*? [Act 4, scene iv]
Rin. Last night a post did bring it S^{r}.
Ber: A weekly poast?
Rin. I S^{r}.
Lan. Brought he no other newes?
Rin: None but *Currants*, & those the printers send a broad
wth as much confidence as a k^{t} oth' poast will sweare.
Ber: Did yor m^{r} write no newes?
Rin: None S^{r} but that wch is newes considering the duch
men & we are all of flesh & blood nere a kin, wch is;
they keep their ancient fashion & state, w^{ch} ‸\constancie/ gets them
com̃endation, but we change o^{r}ꞇ as oft as haberdashers
doe their blocks, & so are counted apes like Englishmen,
if you please yo^{u} may read it, there's nothing in it that

20. [Fol. 215r]

needs to be kept so secret as the intention of a
trades man to breake, nor has a drunken carrier
bene corrupted wth ale, & therefore suffered a proling
informer to breake it open, before it came to the
hands that should receaue it
Ber. Make's he no mention of his return?
Rin. Some ten dayes hence he writes he will be here S^{r}.
Ber 'Tis well; hath *Dianora*, & *Oretta*
Visited my sister lately?
Rin. Not to my knowledge S^{r}. *Enter Oretta & Dianora.*
here they come.
Ber: Weel stand aside & mark their cariage & discourse.
Oret. These elder brothers are the silliest fellowes,
Didst euer see a hobby horse forget buyings so oft?

not this

1470 *Landolpho,*] another comma appears below ^{2}*o* 1472 *post*] *o* blotted; character added above and blotted 1476 *a broad*] = *abroad* 1487 *proling*] *l* possibly poorly formed *b* for *probing* 1496] SP high

Dia. I & had foure aces dealt him & lost the double ruffe.
Oret. Thou sayst true & the first stock he bought
he put out Tom.
Dia. And yet they say this fellow in England is
thought to haue much solid matter in him, &
that his father sent him hither to learn to be
a statesman.
Oret. Heauen grant his fathers bountie slack not, and
weel gleek him I warrant thee, didst thou mark
his breeches, & his Sabees coat?
Dia. The coat hung scuruily I ha' forgot the breeches.
Oret. And the breeches were as scuruy, for they had
no inclination ith' world to the french, & while
that fashion lasts, he that followes it not, deserues
not to weare a periwig, nor a band vnstarcht, &
these are both vsd now by the fashionisticall lords.
Ber: Saue yo^{u} ladies are yo^{u} censuring a man for wearing
his clothes?
Oret. Yes & iudicially S^{r}, Art can discern what ignorance
cannot.
Ber: Me thinks it were a deed of charity
In such as yo^{u} by courteous visitation,
To raise the low brought spirits of *Lisetta*
To some degree of mirth.
Oret. We haue imploy'd
Much time to the same purpose, & she ꝑmised
To leaue of greife till she had cause to vse it.

[Fol. 215v/20v]

W^{ch} I told her she could not haue, vnles her
husband should die, & she be so vnfurnisht of suters
that her age or wrinckled face should barr the
gallants from asking her <~~the~~> ‸\a/ question.
Lan: Doe yo^{u} think this is the way to cheare a woman?
Oret. A way probatum S^{r}, as is written in o^{r} p^{r}seruing
booke, for varietie where it may be had; & where
it may not the thought of varietie will giue a

1499] SP high 1500 *he*] *h* blotted 1502] SP high 1506] SP high 1514 *now*] *w* altered from *n* 1515] SP high 1517] SP high 1519] SP high 1523] SP high 1529 <~~*the*~~>] heavily cancelled 1533 *the*] *t* written over *h*

woman content, & content & muskadine will
make any woman fatt.

Dia. But I feare she's now falling into a relapse, or
worse into a consumption, for of late I heare
she keeps little company wth any but friers.

Lan. I loue her much the better, religious men
Are those we should conuerse wth, for their cariage
should be a rudder to lay peoples actions.

Oret Tis true S^{r}, but to keep much company wth those
that eat but one meale a day; & once a weeke
nether flesh nor any thing that comes of flesh
is ill phisick for a weake woman, except they by
a figure p^{r}scribe her to doe quite contrary to what
they doe, & as they auoid flesh, so she should pursue
it, & as they eschue it, so she should imbrace it louingly.

Ber: I am sorry she's so well acquainted wth yo^{u},
And feare yor lightnes may be much iniurious
To her approued chastitie, wch yet
Outlusters yo^{rs} as gold inferiour mettles.

Oret. Witt is seldome in a suit out of fashion, or a head
like yo^{r}c, yor clothes, & yor words come both from the
broker's, farewell & be hang'd. *Ex. Or: & Dia*:

Rin: This is a beast of mettle, a high comer S^{r},
Yet Ile vndertake to giue her the cornish hugg,
And lay her on her back wthout wrestling, strugling,
striuing or crying yo^{u} hurt me, or oh my left leg.

Ber. I verily beleeue she's ith' p^{r}dicament
Of a post horse, ready for any trauell
Allow her but the hire of her stage, but
Rinaldo as yor care hath hitherto

21. [Fol. 216r]

Bene much & so esteemd, so ꝑseuer
In doing yor m^{r} seruice, & vs yor freinds
An acceptable courtesie, let yor strict eyes
Obseruingly discern whether *Lisetta*
Take any pleasure in these courtezans,
Yo^{r} vnsuspected warines may informe

1541 *peoples*] *l* retraced 1553] SP high 1558 *on*] *n* altered from *f*

Yor selfe & vs, when if we should declare
Or selues inquisitours, all wayes would be stopt vp
might giue vs light of any thing is done.
And if we vnderstand by yor aduertisement
Their conuersation may be pr iudiciall
To the credit of or long fam'd family
Lisetta's hor, & *Caquirino*'s trust
Reposd in you & vs, weel run a course
Shall frustrate their intent, & so discharge
His trust & or ingagment.

Rin. No Dayes shall ~~not~~ pass
Nor minutes whose particular expence
Of ~~time~~ ^\howres/ doth make them be denominate
The prodigall vnthrifts of vnrecalled time,
But my care taking comfort in my labour
+ So't may be vsefull to my honour'd master,
And any way behoouefull to my Mistres,
Administring you cause of satisfaction,
Shall not be guilty of the smallest particle
Of time, wherein I doe leaue vnobseru'd
The least conuenience, by wch opportunitie
I may giue light of any thing is needfull.

Lan: The progress of yor life hath giu'n assurance
Of yor approued carefull secrecy
And secret care, therefore multiplication
Of reasons to ꝑswade you to be faithfull
would manifest or weakenes, & fouly iniure
Yor faithfull truth, & true fidelitie.
Therefore or expectation shall sit still
And not looke after any thing, till you
Shall call for it's attention, let vs go in. / *Ex: Be: Lan*: *& Rin*:

Enter Oretta & Lisetta. [Act 4, scene v]

Oret. Why now you carry yor selfe becom̃ingly.

[Fol. 216v/21v]

Lis: Thou sayst true, I can now shorten my coursie, like
| a duches, & if a better man then my father come to

1580 *No*] inserted in L margin before line 1582 ~~*time*~~ ^ *howres/*] caret below *m* of ~~*time*~~ 1597 *fidelitie*] *d* altered

salute me, & be but old and hairie, I turn my cheeke
to him, & tell him I wonder he durst venture abroad
seeing the weather is so vnseasonable, & he so vnfit
for company.

Oret. But according to the varietie of obiects, I hope yo^{u}
know how to alter yor cariage.

Lis. Oh to an haire, I can if occasion serue carry my body
as euen as a court ladie doth when she turns ith'
canaries, but didst not thou heare what an affront
my gown had put vpon it the other day?

Oret. Not I by *Cupids* mother.

Lis: Well remembred, Ile tell thee a prety tale of *Cupid*, doe
but put me in mind when I ha' done this.

Oret. I will, but first for the wrong of yor gown.

Lis. Ile tell thee, because 'twas a colour much vs'd; I bought
me a gown, betwixt a gredeline, a tawny & a decoy, ~~yet~~
not p^{r}cisely any one of the colours, yet had an inclination
to all, & when I had a conceipt no woman vnder a well
fashioned Lady or a lawyers wife of good estimation wou'ld
haue imitated my stuffe, in comes the nimble sawcy knaue
Snip the barber, & in a suite of the very same peece
cries God bless my worship.

Oret. He was too blame if he knew it were of the same peece.

Lis: Nay the rogue stood in't, & said it was no fault, therefore
in discretion I thought it fitt to call him proud Iack=
an apes & let him goe, to teach a rascall how to know
his duty towards his betters another time

Oret. This was well caried & sprightfully, but what now
not y^{is} of *Cupids* curling iron?

Lis. That story is worth thy knowledge, & a chronicle.

Oret. How wast I pray?

Lis: A greater weight hangs on it then to tell
It like some com̄on passage of the world.

Oret. I doe approue yor iudgement, & will not question
The truth of what you speake, yet I must tell yo^{u}
If't be a pleasure you conceale vntold

1620 *yet*] smeared for deletion
r lawyers] *l* altered or retraced

1623 *or*] superscript *r* smeared for deletion above

Yo^{u} wrong me that I am not a partaker
wth yo^{u} in ioy, but if some ill occurrence

22. [FOL. 217r]

Hath crost yor prime delights, yo^{u} wrong my trust
And strong affection, (wch would participate
wth you in all extremes) by this concealement.
Lis. 'Tis a thing would rauish a mettled womans eares
But once to heare related.
Oret. Would it stirr mettle?
Lis: ___ Did I but think thou wouldst keep councell, I
Would tell thee allmost a miracle, wch was wrought
By the sweet god himselfe.
Oret. It is my trade
Sometimes to act in silence, & I can hold.
Lis: Since then I know, the greatest priuiledges
Beare no esteeme, vntill a generall notion
And approbation seale their worth by triall
Wth any but the persons that inioy them;
Ile let yo^{u} know a thing, wch when yo^{u} heare
" will yeeld you cause of wonder, & produce
". Enuy in others, whose inferiour beauties
May take fraile men, not captiuate the gods.
The glorious Archer wth his fatall bow
And quiuer at his back last night descended
In mortall shape, & wth a protestation,
W^{ch} could not be dissembled, did assure me
The eminent perfections of *Lisetta*
This way made happy, haue made so deep impression
In the affection of his Soueraigne Deitie
That he renounc'd his supreme seat of state
And trod on earth assuming humane shape
Onely to tast my beautie.
Oret. Can this be true?
Lis: ___ As I am a woman this is most infallible
For many nights I haue inioy'd his p^{r}sence
In such a full perfection that euery time
My thoughts contemplate of his youthfull actiuenes
It pleases me extremely.

1644 *w^{ch}*] pen stroke after *h*   1656 *approbation*] *b* retraced

Oret. I beleeue yo^{u}, & enuie yor felicitie as a yong wench
that when a maried couple are im bedded
lies ith' next chamber to them & gnawes the sheets
Because tis not her night, farewell *Lisetta*,
Those that are hungrie & haue their stomacks sharp
Need not more prouocation.
Lis. *Rinaldo.* *Enter Rinaldo*

[Fol. 217v/22v]

Rin. No. busines is so earnest can detaine
me from attending yor obserued call
Lis: Go to frier *Albert*, & tell him if his leisure
Will grant a visitation libertie
Ile p^{r}sently come see him. *Exit Rinaldo.*
not y^{is}—— How much more nimble is *Cupid* then my husband!
They wrong him much that say he is a boy.
For I'm sure he hath a lustie able back
And proues himselfe a complet man in action.
I heard a Poet say I am acquainted wth,
Saturn deposed got Iupiter the name
Of power & vsurpation, *Mercury*
Is fam'd among the gods for winged speed;
Mars & *Bellona* for their power in warr
The timorous people feare, Diuine *Apollo*
Shewes his prophetique power by foretelling
Euents to come & knotty things disclosure
But of all the gods giue me sweet *Cupid*.
Enter Albert in his study & Rinaldo.
Alb. Lady you'r wellcome, yor vouchafed visit
Names me yor seruant, please yo^{u} sit down & rest. *they sit.*
Yo^{r} man may if he will ith' other roome
Take his repose. *Ex: Rinaldo.*
Lis: I euer must acknowledge
The fauour I haue tasted of, the fruit
Of yor direction, & much bewaile those women
That liue in purr=blind ignorance, debarrd
The benefitt of light, because they haue not some
Discerning man may set them in a way,

1701 *disclosure*] *l* written over another character 1702 *gods*] *d* altered 1710 *much*] *u* written over *a*

To app^{r}hend such benefitts; the conuersation
Yo^{u} daignd to haue wth me hath gott yo^{u} ho^{r},
And wth a liberall extent afforded
me things aboue expression; for the god
As yo^{u} foretold clad in a glorious habit
Last night appear'd, & by such certain tokens
Error cannot express, hath giu'n assurance
Of what yor sage p^{r}diction did foretell.

Alb. We that know truth, & shew it to the simple
Spend all o^{r} dayes in studie, to no end
But onely to gaine knowledge, whereby we may
Inform mens anxious soules of abstruse doubts,

23. [Fol. 218r]

And should not what we speake succeed, o^{r} words
Would seeme delusions, & o^{r} feigning tongs
But messengers of lying consequence.

Lis: Yo^{u} need not striue to force a more beleefe
In me then I haue of yor great sufficiencie.
The god himselfe approu'd yor words, & what
Yo^{u} spake his reall actions seal'd for truth

Alb. I was selected as a messenger
To let yo^{u} know his mind, & him yor answer,
And faithfully perform'd that trusty office,
Nor since that time haue bene at all acquainted
wth passages betwixt yo^{u}; but this I know,
No sooner had he lent his gracious hearing
not y^{is} To intertain yor answer & his ioy,
But I perceau'd my soule to leaue my body
And twinckle in the aire as *Cesars* did
When ~~cou~~ courteous *Venus* bore it vp to heauen,
And to my thinking was transferr'd by elues
And fairies to those plesure yeelding feelds
About *Eliziũ*, where the soules of men
That died for loue now haue their happy residence,
To tell yo^{u} how this metempsacosis
Or wondrous transmigration was effected
Expression is vnable; or how my body

1742 ~~*cou*~~] smeared for deletion 1747 *metempsacosis*] *a* altered

was from that place where *Cupid* ‸\did/ imploy it
wholly in yor seruice translated hither
we may inquire, but must remaine vnsatisfied
Vntill we can ascend to high discoueries.

Lis: They are vnworthy of the meanest benefitts
That doe not app^r^hend them, & those againe
That prise great fauours as they should be valued
not y^is^ Recompence in inioyeing; yor cleare discern
(Exprest in what you felt) hath differenc'd
Yo^r^ acceptation from a misconceipt.
And yor deepe iudgem^t^ from a weake capacitie.

Alb: Yo^u^ giue a courteous censure, & I confess
My body nere inioy'd a complete happines
But in this blest imployment, *He takes a book down*
I vnderstand *& lookes in it*
By reuelation, that the god will come
Againe before't be long, & if he should

[FOL. 218v/23v]

At his appearance find yo^u^ not wth in
Perhaps hee'l be displeas'd.

Lis. Ile leaue yo^u^ S^r^
And wth a due obseruance wait his coming

Alb. Yo^u^ take the cue ingeniously, & I profess
not y^is^ I haue not dealt wth such an app^r^hension.

Fin: Act: 4. *Exeunt.*

Act 5. Enter Bergamino, Landolpho, & Rinaldo. [Act 5, scene i]

Rin. My intelligence hath giu'n me an assurance
That the curtezans haue promised this day
To call my m^ris^, & they three together
Must goe abroad vnto a womans feast.

Enter Oretta & Dianora.

Oret. You're well met gentlemen, how doth o^r^ freind *Lisetta*?

Rin: I think she is hardly vp yet.

Dia. O how she is improou'd, she had wont to be
Betimes ith' morning vp among her maids.
To see the dusty slatterns cleanse the roomes.

Oret. Then she wore scuruie clothes.

1757 *inioyeing*] *e* possibly altered 1780 *met*] *m* altered

Ber: And is improu’d say you because she now lies
long ~~<in’ a>~~ ‸ \a’/ bed.
Dia. Yes, & Ile stand to’t, she is much improu’d
In vnderstanding, if she obserue this course
And another rule I taught her, wch. is
After her first sleep to haue a maudlin cup
Furnisht wth eggs & muskadine, or if you’l haue
The vsuall phrase, a nourishing cold caudle,
W^{ch} when her stomack stands to she may sup of,
Though’t be but a midwifes draught a quart, or so,
Then sleep againe, & by this wholesome drink
And sleeping after’t in a constant course
Shee’l make her cheeks grow plump, & where there’s /flesh\
’Tis possible to lay a gracefull colour.
Lan: Good huswiues sleep not when the Sun is vp
Nor get their flesh wth ease, but ere the cock
Giue warning to the sluggish clown to rise
They call their seruants vp, & in compassion
Of the hard labour they are going to
Prepare their earned breakfast
Dia. I pray what then?
Lan: And thus get good report, & the repute

24 [Fol. 219r]

Of being discreet wise mothers of their families.
Oret. What wth making milk porrege for the carters?
Ber: By vnderstandingly disposing of
The house affaires, & ordering all things neatly.
Oret. Can a woman shew more neatnes, then in dressing
her selfe handsomely, frousing her haire down
o’ the french fashion, drying it wth powder of a good
sent, pinning her past bord band backward enough
tying her slasht sleeues wth chamlet or raine bow
ribben of the same her girdle is on, & then in
wearing thin gloues next her hand & spanish o’ th’ top.
Lan: | These are phrases the golden age nere heard of
Oret. | And the golden age was rich but not well bred,

1790 *w^{ch}*.] stop possibly accidental ink spot 1795 *Though’t*] a downstroke for *t* after *h*, false start; replaced by *t* 1798 */flesh*] insertion preceded by square L bracket to separate it from text on ll. 1799–1800

for as I haue heard (in those dayes *Venice* & *London*
were both vnbuilt, & those are the places where
women may get most knowledge how to carry
themselues.

Lan: Now yo^{u} talk of *Venice* & of *London*, 'pray what
newes doe yo^{u} heare from thence, yo^{u} goe so much
abroad you're not vnfurnisht.

Oret. We heare from thence that tradesmen breake
to get by't.

Rin: 'Tis true one of my acquaintance did so, & the
yong rogues vse it most, that when they haue
cheated their creditours, they may set vp
againe wth a greater stock then they began at first.

Ber: Doth *Venice* yeeld no wonders like to this?

Oret. Yes & more strange, *Dianora* & my selfe came
not y^{is} lately from a wedding, & now are going to a
churching, both the works of propagation,
& she heard newes but I did know't before.

Ber: What is yor newes a riddle, 'tis so obscure?

Dia: Tis a riddle, & 'tis not a riddle, & yet tis a riddle too.

Lan: Hy da, backward & forward like a horse in a rode?

Oret. Come, come, the truth is, *Cupid* lay wth *Lisetta* a night
or two agoe, & hath got her wth child of a little god.

Ber: Out yo^{u} damn'd whore, slander my sister?

Lan: Make her a strumpet?

Ber: Let's cut her throate.

[FOL. 219v/24v]

Lan: Agreed.

Oret. Hold as yo^{u} loue a woman, & be perswaded
I am not fearefull of the stiffest blade
The stoutest man in *Venice* beares a bout him.
Nor doe yo^{u} think my strong imagination
Hath coyn'd this lye, & then inioyn'd my tong
To vent ~~i<s>~~ it as a truth; but be assur'd
Something like *Cupid* often visitts her;
W^{ch} makes vs many times to want her company
Nor doe I tell you this in vnderualuing

1828] SP high to *it* then deleted   1850 *beares*] retraced   *a bout*] = *about*   1853 ~~*i<s>*~~] ~~*i<s>*~~ possibly altered

Lisetta's worth but for her reputation
For 'tis a credit to haue a god to lye wth one.
If yo^{u} doubt this Ile set yo^{u} in a way
(So you'l be thankfull for't) shall certifie
You fully of this truth.
Ber: I know yor mind. *Giues her mony.*
Here's that makes the lawyer speak! On now.
Oret. This day we haue appointed to be merry in,
And she to goe a long, now if she come not
Doe but attend a while, & ten to one
not y^{is} { You shall see a god descend from heauen to tast
The sweetnes of her body. Ile knock at dore
And if she doe not come think o' my words. *Knocks*
Are you vp freind! Not yet ready *Lisetta*? *Enter Obe*:
Ob: My m^{ris} is not well & takes't vnkindly
You breake her of her sleep.
Oret. I p^{r}thee goe in, & tell her she forgets her selfe,
and if we stay too long the midwife will be gone &
then we shall heare no newes
Ob: I will. *Exit Obedience.*
Ber: 'Tis not a safe thing to put confidence
In yo^{u} that are so mercenary; lately
You seem'd to prise my sisters credit, as if
Yo^{r} life & it had touchd both in one point,
And now for couetous desire of gaine
Yo^{u} would betray her as if it were most co$\tilde{m}$endable
To murther any whose death may bring yo^{u} profitt.
Oret. Yo^{r} ~~<argu>~~ argument's too harsh, & yor strict censure
Is both vnmannerly, & Satyricall;
not y^{is} | Yet we that are knights yonger daughters must
Or trade abroad or marry clarks or butlers

4 25 [FOL. 220r]

| Or some inferiour seruingmen, for o^{r} portions
| Are both so small, & so long time in paying
By reason of charges on o^{r} brothers land~~<...>~~
Compounding for his wardship, & <issu>ing his liuery

1865 *a long*] *along* 1873 *tell*] *e* written over *l* 1884 ~~<*argu*>~~] smeared and blotted 4] slightly smeared, possibly for deletion 25] ink dot above 2 1890 *land*~~<...>~~] ~~<...>~~ seemingly inked out 1891 <*issu*>*ing*] <*issu*> altered and blotted

That the interest of the principall detein'd
will not pay for the making a french gowne.
Therefore to haue repelled the courtesie
Yo^{r} loue did offer had bene a strange neglect
To yo^{u} & shew of ignorance in vs.
And if yo^{u} misaccept the light we giue yo^{u}
Of what *Lisetta* ~~did~~ doth, misapp^{r}hension
will make pure things seeme but adulterate
And all desert vnworthy. *Enter Obedience.*
Ob: My m^{ris} doth intreat you & the company
You're going to, you'l please t' excuse her absence,
because she tooke a p^{r}paratiue last night, to day
must purge & to morow bleed ith' foot. *Exit.*
Oret We wish her phisick good success, *Landolpho*
we are yor seruants & yor *Bergamino.* *Ex: Oret. & Dian:*
Ber: It is impossible such a thing as this
Should be rais'd wthout some ground, 'tmay be she stayes
As *Oretta* did suggest to intertaine
Something like *Cupid*, ~~w^{ch}~~ ^ \but/ if he doe a ppeare
Ile clip his siluer wings & make him die
Like a carion crow.
Lan: we can suspect
no less & 'twill not be amiss a while
T'obserue the dores, & all the passages
Wth those that enter at them.
Rin: Yo^{u} propose a course
not y^{is} Vnquestionably good, & I can set yo^{u}
In a secret place whence yo^{u} may see all accidents
And yet be vnobseru'd.
Ber: That's excellent.
Rin: Please yo^{u} goe in this is the very place. *Ex. they stand aside hidden.*
Enter Friar Albert, & Ricciardo wth an inuentory.
Alb: The Catholick cause will euer bless yor paines
Ricc: Yo^{u} shall see the Inuentory, & all the particulars specified
Alb: What is the totall?
Ricc: Two thousand pounds.

1897 *giue*] *i* written over *a* 1898 *did*] smeared for deletion 1905] SP high 1907] SP high 1910 *w^{ch}*] written above *but* and smeared for deletion *a ppeare*] = *appeare* 1920 *And*] *d* possibly altered 1922 *Ex.*] slightly smeared

Alb: How much to vs?
Ricc: You shall heare, giuen to the holy conuent of *Franciscan Cor=*
deliers in *Venice*, nineteene hundred pound.

[FOL. 220v/25v]

Alb: Is the mony in good mens hands?
Ric: Very good mens hands, for all the debters are ether noble
men, knights, or esquires, except one grasier, who owes an
hundred pound, & a courtier fifty.
Alb. Wee'l nere question the grasier, for those kind of men
seldome break their word or their day, & that makes them
grow so wealthie, but the Lords & the courtiers are the
worst debters.
Ric: They are ho:^{ll} & will doe no man wrong.
Alb. I know not that, but I am sure their honour is their
best securitie, & ~~s~~<when that failes> no body will trust 'hem,
& when courtiers are so farr in debt they dare not
shew their heads, they get a protection royall, & that
barrs all their creditours; I can assure yo^{u} I heard a
Scriuener say that dealt much, he fear'd no mony so
much as that wch was in Lords hands, that he accoun
ted desperate debt
Ric: ~~Itm~~ to &c.
Alb: Neuer repeat more Items; Doth any thing els
concern o^{r} particular?
Ric: No, the rest is to vnnecessary vses, maintaining
his wife & children.
Alb: Then weel neuer trouble o^{r} selues wth reading, thus
farr it doth express what belongs to vs?
Ric: I.
Alb: Then thus farr think vpon & slight the rest,
For this is a rule, we are bound to receaue & to lay
out, but especially to receaue, & as o^{r} receipts must
be carefully performed, so o^{r} layings out must be duly
Disbursed to o^{r} agents in other countries, though
—." they be but french cookes, & dancers in shew, & preists
& Iesuits in practise, such as *Gondomour* imployed in —
—, yo^{u} haue done very well, make yor paines known

1941 *&*] retraced *<when that failes>*] written over smeared deletion 1951] SP high
1963 *done*] *e* blotted

to the superiour, & no question yor reward will be according
to yor desert; I haue a little occasion to speake wth a Lady
hard by, & no man can tell my tale so well as my selfe,
therefore I desire you'l walk before Ile ou^{r}take yo^{u} p^{r}sent<ly>.
This fellow hath done a most meritorious act *Ex. Ric:*
giuen vs all he had, ~~h~~and left his freinds beggars,
why should we not as well com̃and their estates on earth,
as perswade them they cannot come to heauen wthout o^{r}
licence, & as well be masters of their mony as of their wiues?
the reason is, O^{r} power's supreme & they are ignorant.
Avoyd yo^{u} robes of grauitie, I am

26. [FOL. 221r]

T'incounter youth & beautie in a forme *puts of*
More glorious farr then yor⊏, did not you ‸\cloak/ *his habit.*
My plesure=yeelding sin wth shew of holines
Yo^{r} length were of no vse, & my delights
not y^{is} — would be as soone discouered as inioyed
An amorous courtier could not haue wrought his ends,
His sprusenes would haue raisd suspition,
But holy ‸\~~down loo~~ graue look'd/ men are of vnquestion'd credit
And therefore not suspected, though their sins
Outweigh the greatest rorers; Shall I conuince
My selfe of that I'm going to, & barr
My lust of what it longs for,? this would shew
My conscience is weake=stomack't, & dare not let
My body tast incomparable beautie
For feare of clogging it wth guiltines.
These thoughts are scarrcrowes to vnspirited men
But cannot fright a grand proficient.
wth appetitious hast Ile seize my prey. *He knocks.*
Obedience lookes out then returns, speaks.

Ob: M^{ris}, the loueliest man, & the finest clothes, sure it is
he yo^{u} lookt for. *Lisetta lookes out, speakes.*

Lis: It is indeed, goe you down into the kichin, & there
make a foole, & rather then not doe it well stay
an hower about it.

Ob: I know yor mind *Exit Obedience. / Enter Lisetta.*

1969 *had,*] *d* altered from *t*; comma inserted

Alb: The weake & fraile mortalitie of men
Makes their vowes subiect to vnconstant change
And all their deeds vnstable, but the gods
Neuer speak word from their ꝓphetique mouths
W^{ch} the succession of their preostents
Stamps not wth seale of truth. *Cupid* came downe
And at his first appearance gaue a signe
A god was come, wch infallible experience
Made yo^{u} beleeue, & if yor mistrust
Caus'd by some misinforming doubt suggest
He not esteemes yo^{u} as his promise tyed
\+ | His Deitie at first; yor able eyes
| May by their cleare distinction satisfie
not y^{is} | You here he stands before yo^{u}, & other senses
\+ | Though not so noble yet sometimes more pleasing
Make yo^{u} confess by feeling, I'm as actiue
Sprightly & strong as when yo^{u} first made triall

Enter from behind Ber: & Landolpho.

Ber: Out yo^{u} damnd slaue is this yor holines?

[Fol. 221v/26v]

Ile cut yor sacred throat. *Albert takes the sword from Bergamino*
Alb. You will not sure?
Ile pick yor enuious teeth, & make yo^{u} know
'Tis not a safe thing to oppose o^{r} pleasure. *Excurrit Alb.*
Ber: Help, help, help, *Rinaldo* help. *Enter Rinaldo running.*
Rin: All the house but Obedience & I are gone abroad, not so much as the kitchin boy but scowr'd his dishes betimes, such sport is vpon the *Rialto*, as neuer was seene.
Lan: But I am sure at home is the tragedie of yor m^{ris} credit
The vtter ruine of yor m^{rs} house
And the renowne of o^{r} till now vnquestion'd
Family, smothered in disgracefull ashes.
Ber: was this yor sicknes sister? this yor phisick?
Yo^{r} bleeding i'the foot the base depression
Of the friers adulterat body?
Lis. 'Twas not the frier.
Lan. ~~'Tw~~ Who was't the deuill?

2000 *of*] horizontal stroke through top of *f* 2022 *Alb.*] written in darker ink; possibly added later
2035 ~~'Tw~~] smeared for deletion *was't*] something smeared to R of apostrophe

Lis: ’Twas *Cupid* in the friers shape.
Ber. And is this *Cupids* vestm^{t}? ’pray yo^{u} looke; *points to the friars habit.*
Cupid weares gray & is a Cordelier?
You are abus’d & we, & yo^{u} shall die for’t.
And when by this kind of expiation
Yo^{u} haue quit the world of such a sinfull creature
As now inioyes the benefitt of aire
But shall not long, then the auersation
Of heauens due punishment implor’d on humble knees
Perhaps may be procur’d from vs & all
The members of yor kinred, & therefore, die. *Offers to strangle her.*
Lan. Let Iustice take reuenge, & heauen it selfe
Dropp thunderbolts as thick as haile or snow
On her offending head, but not o^{r} hands
Be so p^{r}sumptuous as vsurp it’s office
Lis: Patience & mercy are a kin, & yo^{u}
Are both my brothers, let my penitent tong
Craue but attention from yor courteous eares
To what I shall declare, & if yor iudgement
Will not be altered by ꝑswasiue reasons
To grant me a repriue, my obuious neck
Shall meet yor furie, & willingly receaue
Those strokes yor axe of anger shall inflict.
Rin: ’Tis the duty of an vpright iudge to heare
And then determin, & not to mulct the partie
Before he see his fault declar’d apparently.
You doe suspect & ’tis but a suspition,
Suspend yor censure till yo^{u} know the truth

27. [Fol. 222r]

W^{ch} neuer iniures any. *Enter Obedience.*
Ob: My M^{r} is returned, for two sailers
Calld pitch & cording fellowes that stink of tarre
Are at the ware house dore, & haue brought his trunks. *Ex:*
Rin. This happy newes calls for my carefull p^{r}sence
Wth=in to make things handsome, & prepare
The house in such a decent correspondencie
As may declare my diligence, & answer

2051 *a kin*] = *akin*   2061 *apparently*] *e* altered from *a*

A so long ~~M~~^{rs} absent m^{rs} expectation.
Yet since my selfe hath soly bene acquainted
(Except yo^{u} two,) wth the breaking out
Of this ill accident, let my meane aduise
Enter yor eares, & if yo^{u} find it weightie
And worthy to be follow'd, make it vsefull
for this occasion, if not accept it as
The fruit of well intending seruice, w^{ch}
Neuer is blam'd for insufficiencie.
My m^{ris} craues yor patience, & desires
You'l heare her own relation, & if this proue
As all we wish it may, she's in no fault;
If the worst yor feare lookes for doe appeare
+ Smother it in discretion, & let it not
Be openly expos'd to enuious viewe
Whose malice will delight in her hard chance.
My duty caus'd the herald of my mind
To be thus bold, & now I craue yor pardon. *Exit.*
Lis: Reason must hearken to all propositions
That suit so wth indifferencie as this,
And you must not retaine the name of brothers
Or els admitt this course; yor free leaue granted,
I will explain the in side of my heart
Wth an vnfeign'd confession; my husband gone
And I depriu'd at once of him & all
The happines his p^{r}sence did afford;
A number of my freinds considering
The greefe lay heauy on me did compasionate
My sad retir'dnes, & tender of my health
(W^{ch} they knew melancholy would impare)
Did often come to see me, among w^{ch}
Albert (surnam'd of *Imola* he came from)
Did visit me in courteous charitie
And told me 'twas a dangerous thing to lie
Alone for feare of sprights, wch I beleeu'd
And he confirm'd wth strong asseuerations

2094 *in side*] = *inside* 2104 *Did*] *D* altered from *d*

[Fol. 222v/27v]

Yet said, because my beautie did transcend.
All other womens that he knew, 'twas fitt
My bedfellow should be of great desert,
And did affirm that he had found by reading
Cupid himselfe desir'd this priuiledge
And I must not denie him, yet since his glory
not y^{is} | was more then humane, & a womans weakenes
Could ‸ \not/ abide him in his height of strength
Because he was immortall, if I would
Appoint the shape he should come to me in
He would assume it, but it was most conuenient
To come in frier *Alberts*, wch I granted
Not in respect of any loose desire
But 'cause I know both you & I & all
The cittie must wth a strong beleefe giue credit
To what he saith as most authenticall.
not y^{is} | If notwthstanding all this you conclude
Me an offendo^{r}, I yeeld to yor decree,
Yet I will stand to't 'twas a religious errour
Soly occasiond by the friers procurement.
Ber: All the weake faults of ignorance inuoke
pitty & not reuenge, & when a thing
Is past recall, folly doth wish't vndone.
Lan: 'Tis true, &'tis a point of good discretion
To smother things wch being brought to light
Will bring the curious searchers greefe & shame,
for ill things stirrd euer infect them soonest
That rake in troubled ashes;
Lis: Yo^{u} conceiue
The thing aright, & since auspicious heauen
Hath brought my husband back, conceale my fault
~~Conceale my fault, & let him not perceaue it~~
And let him not perceaue it, but since my honour
Hath suffered by the friers wickednes
Let him haue his desert whose base ꝑswasion
Drew me to this foule sin.
~~*Lan*~~ *Ber*. Yo^{r} iust request

2115 *not*/] interlined in darker ink 2139] smeared for deletion 2144 ~~*Lan*~~] smeared for deletion

weel think of & performe, yet 'cause the order
He's ^ \of/ co$\tilde{m}$nands respectiue reuerence
From vs & all men, weel conceale o^{r} wrong
Till we can catch him in the priuate walks
Belonging to the conuent, where reuenge
May giue ^ \ him/ his desert, & we vnknown

28 [FOL. 223r]

Discharge o^{r} duty, wch yo^{u} iniur'd call for.

Lis: My greefe oppressed soule returns yo^{u} thanks,
And I intreat you'l grant me one more fauour
W^{ch} is that all we wth alacritie
May entertaine my safe returned husband
wthout the least appearance of disquiet
In yo^{u}, & thus you'l doe/a gratefull office
To me wch I can nere requite.

Lan: Wee'l not deny yor fitt desire, since he's not farr of
The sailers brought his things long since. *Ex: Oẽs.*

Enter Albert wounded & Zeppa. [Act 5, scene ii]

Alb: As yo^{u} haue bene an able man in yor youth,
& then did know what accidents vsed to befall
men that youthfull occasions drew abroad in the
night time pitty the distres of one faint wth bleeding

Zeppa. Is this a time of night to call men out of their beds?

Alb: The compulsion of necessitie is a reason for what is ~~done~~,
done, & had I not bene abus'd by drunken rogues & so
come to this mischance, yo^{u} had rested still in quiet.

Zep: Let him that hurt yo^{u} heale yo^{u}, for I doe not mean
to entertain yo^{u}, how if some robbery haue bene co$\tilde{m}$itted
to night, & the officers should search & find yo^{u} i' my
house, would you ha' me hang for company?

Alb: There's no such thing I assure yo^{u}.

Zep: Tis more nor I know, here are strange signes, yo^{u}
ha' fine cloes me thinks, & few ha so mich siluer o' their
sutes i'theese dayes, but those that ether steale vm
or owe for vm, & therefore I desire to be excus'd,
neuer any man shall come wthin my durrs nor warm

2157 *doe/a*] / inserted to indicate word division 2167 *~~done~~*] smeared for deletion 2169 *yo^{u} had*] *y* altered and superscript *u* inserted; *u* smeared above *h* 2172 *to night*] = *tonight* 2175 *yo^{u}*] superscript *u* smeared

him before my aster, that con not giue an account how he cam by's cloes.

Alb. × Come, come old father, I'l shew yo^{u} the old mans god [*shewes mony*], & that I am sure will work?

Zep: Will hurden sheets serue yo^{u}?

Alb: Any thing till morning, I desire onely a rag to tye my wound; & a roome to put my head in till it be day, & then Ile trouble yo^{u} no longer.

Zep: Well vpon condition goe in there.

Alb: I thank yo^{u} heartily.

Zep: Nay houd a little tine, houd a little tine, by th' feck o' my body yo mun pey afore yo goen in, as the fellow made me for seeing the Olephant. that catches appowes wi's nose. [*Alb: giues him mony.*]

[FOL. 223v/28v]

Well now goe in, & occupy any thing but my daughter.

Hacten^{s} | . An this be not sum kneeght Ile be hang'd, he's so loth to pay rent for his chaumber, or it may 'tis won o' th' gentlemen that went the last voyage he made him so good cloes to loose his blood in, yet he thought they were too braue to be killd in, & therefore when he saw there was any daunger, he made him selfe a free pass wth his heeles & run away, & so came whome again much ~~more~~ wiser nor he went, warrs & experience teach a mon many straunge things. *Ent: Oret: & Dia:*

Oret. Well mett old father, what newes where yo^{u} dwell?

Zep: Yo^{u} know not where I dwell, & don yo^{u} ask what newes there?

Oret. Why 'tis no matter where yo^{u} dwell, if yo^{u} dwell vnder heauen, I'm sure there's newes where yo^{u} dwell, for if Yo^{u} dwell i the citty, yo^{u} may heare trades men repine at the strangenes & vnconstancie of the time, & that is newes to those that haue known better dayes; & if Yo^{u} ~~like~~ ‸\liue/ i'the suburbs, yo^{u} may heare whores complaine they cannot get houses to exercise their occupation in, because gentlemens wiues that come out of the country take vp all the lodgings, & that's newes to

2182] SP high 2192 *Olephant*] *O* written over *e* 2195 *An*] *A* written over *O* 2196 *pay*] *y* altered 2203 *many*] *man* altered 2208 *Yo^{u}*] written over *The* *dwell*] *d* written over *g* 2211 ~~*like*~~ ‸*liue*/] caret below *e* of ~~*like*~~

their simple husbands that keep home in the country

Zep: The greatest newes I know is ’tis strange to see gentlewomen o’ yor fashion abrode so late.

Dia. Yo^{u} speake like an old man ’twas not so when yo^{u} were Yong

Zep: No truly, my lonlady was counted a very good huswife, & she wud euer goe’t bed betime that she meeght rise betime.

Oret. That was the beggers fashion, did she not weare a border & a french hood

Zep: I think she had a thing on her head she call’d a whood.

Oret. I told yo^{u} so, how witty are o^{r} times!, In my conceit there’s no weare to yor frisled dress, & yor frenchlawn bands; for they will wash but once, & therefore the citizens wiues will not haue them.

Zep: And mee thinks of all & of all, a faire partlet about a womans neck, & a kerchew vpon her hyead, & an apron wth a lace so it be thin that the red peticote may shew thorow it better by odds then that gown my yong londlords wife had on, when I went last to carry my rent, for hoo

29. [FOL. 224r]

had a gyowne on had sleeues, & appurn o’ won colour, & back & skurts of another.

Dia: Goe old man get yo^{u} to yor beads, those & a good fire are best for yo^{u}

Zep: Indeed now I think’t on’t tis time to be gwon, for I haue a guest a whome has better cloes, nor any o’ yo’ ha, & one fashion that I nere saw sicher, he has things like whings on his shoulders.

Oret. Some direct french wing.

Zep: French or English I know not, ’tis as big as’t lap o’my coat, & he has a quiuer hangs at’s back, & a shaft in’s codpeece.

Oret. What will yo^{u} ‸ \say/ if it be *Cupid* that visits *Lisetta* so often?

Zep: That cannot be, my wench has a ballet she lurns to

2221 *wud*] *u* altered 2226 *times!,*] *!* possibly inserted 2228 *once*] *c* altered 2231 *kerchew*] ^{2}*e* altered 2232 ^{2}*it*] *t* altered from *s* 2247 *yo^{u}* ‸ *\say/*] caret below superscript *u* of *yo^{u}*

sing a neeghts, & in that ballet *Cupid is calld a prety*
little boy, & therefore it cannot be he. *En: Ber: & Land:*
Oret: It may be he for all this here come two can tell vs more.
Ber: Did ‸ \you/ not see one goe this way in a siluer suit, a quiuer
at his back, a scarfe ouer his eyes, & a sword in his hand.
Zep: Why dee ye ash?
Lan: Men that are wrong'd haue cause to ask many questions
For w^{ch}, their iniurie must not giue a reason
To any, but their own sad thoughts in priuate.
Zep. Indeed now yo^{u} rubb vp my remembry, there was sich
a thing did call me vp, & I ha' ladg'd him, but he sayes
he must be gwon at day breake.
Ber: Do yo^{u} know frier *Alberts* face?
Zep: I think I doe.
Ber: Is it not he?
Zep: He's of his stature & resemble's him very mich in's face.
Lan: Will yo^{u} let vs see him?
Zep: It may be I cannot.
Lan: O that yo^{u} could, you should not name the thing
We would not doe by way of recompence.
Zep: Ile doe my best, & if you'l pay me well, 'tis the deel to
a groat but Ile help you to th' speech on him.
Lan: What will yo^{u} ask & whither will yo^{u} bring him?
Zep: Some ten grotes & two pence, or such a like thing in
hand ‸ \& two cowes gresse as long as <.>yo & I liue, together/ &
if I doe not bring him yo^{u} hither wthin this hower
Ile send you word to th' contrary, & you'st ha' yor mony againe.
Lan: Yo^{u} say well, I desire no more here's yor mony.
Zep: This mony's quickly earn'd, & my wife will thank me for her
cow gate. *Exit*.

[Fol. 224v/29v]

Oret: Will you beleeue me another time?
Lan: Experience, the scoole mistres of fooles, & the executioner of
vnhappy men, hath made vs know too well the abuse yo^{u}
gaue vs notice of.
Oret. In womens businesses we are able sometimes to tell more
then ether wisards or wise men.

2252 *Did* ‸ *\you/ not*] caret below *n* of *not* 2259 *thing*] *in* altered 2264 *in's*] *s* altered
2273 *hand* ‸ *\& … together/*] caret below *d* of *hand*

Lan: Shall I desire a fauour from yo^{u}, wch is y^{t} you will keepe
councell, & allthough the thing is as bad as may be,
Yet if it be hidden wth concealement, that it may not
come to my brothers eare, who is now returnd safe
home, I doe not think but all will be as well as is
possible in such a bad matter, & ^ \as/ according to the φuerb
what the eye sees not the heart greeues not, so
certainly what is kept from his knowledge will not
trouble his mind.

Dia: A very good motion, & yo^{u} shall find vs ith' same mind
the Iustice of peace was that had a man brought before
him for lying wth another mans wife, & because he could
not perswade the cornuto to be quiet, told him that
it was no hurt if his seale ring had bene vpon his
clerks finger, wch tooke the fellow so extremely, that he
said it was fitt he should be ruled by worp:^{ll} comparisons,
this is a way to quiet him, if it should chance to come
to his knowledge, but if it doe not weel be as merry
as at a gossiping, & for more security talke, as most
women doe, nothing to the purpose.

Lan: You'l doe <.> a thankfull office, 'pray let's goe in to bid him
wellcome from his tedious iourny; but howsoeuer
haue a care of the maine.

Oret. I warrant yo^{u} weel carry o^{r} busines as closely as a cutpurse.

Enter Albert & Zeppa. *Ex. ões.* [Act 5, scene iii]

Zep: Yo^{u} cannot scape but in some strange disguise, for there
is as much inquiring after yo^{u}, as for an honest lawyer
or a kneeght in execution, but this I dare vndertake,
that if you will but stand to the hazard of the co͂mon
peoples violence, one quarter of an hower, you shall
after that be brought whome to the monasterie vn=
known & wthout danger.

Alb: Ile aduenture to vndergoe both a greater perill, & a
punishment of more continuance, so ^ \yo^{u}/ will but assure me
the success shall be answerable to yor promise & my
expectation.

2295 *wife*] line drawn above *wi*   2304 <.>] blotted

30. [Fol. 225r]

Zep: not y^{is} How sen yo^{u} by this? I haue a son that is a tanner of cunnieskins, or in a more soft & mannerly phrase a furrier, & the Dukes beare‸\ward/ some quarter of a yeare since lost his great beare, & sold his skin to my son wch he drest wth the hyaire on, & keeps it in his shop as potecaries doe their boxes wth great words vpon vm, & nothing in vm, onely to make country people beleeue, they can kill men as easily as a farrier can doe a horse that is sick of a cold, & this skin Ile vndertake to doe yo^{u} a kindnes yo^{u} shall ha', wch when yo^{u} ha' put on will couer yo^{u} all ore, & yo^{u} may goe where yo^{u} wull vnknowne.

Alb: You meane to put some gull vpon me, for this will Draw such a company of boyes & doggs together, & theyl be so busy about me that I shall be in more danger then if I exposd my selfe to the rage of my greatest enimies.

Zep: Sha, it shall be p^{r}sently after one a clock, when the boyes dare not be from schoole vpon paine o' whipping, & I am so well acqu<~~a~~>‸\a/inted wth the buchers, (since it pleased m^{r} warden I thank his ‸\worpp/ to let my wife ha' the place of tripe scraper,) that I'le intreat them to keep vp all their hard bitten currs, & let none not y^{is} loose but curteous, kind, & well behaued dogs, such as are like a bribed Iudge, that will bark very fiercely, but not bite at all.

Alb: This cannot be done, for the skin will not be bigg enough to couer my hands feet & all, & when the vnruly rout doe but <~~.n~~> once, \<~~s..~~>/ perceaue, or suspect they haue a tric‸\k/~~k~~, put vpon 'vm, they'l be as angrie as a gallant that's cousen'd on's whore.

Zep: Ile answer yo^{u} for that too, for this day we obserue as a merry festiuall, & 'tis lawfull for ony mon to disguise a mon in the skin of a beare or any forme of bett^{r} deuise, wch being done he mun bring him vpon S^{t} marks market place, whence after two courses he may take him away, wthout rendring a reason for what he did, or giue=

2322 *beare‸\ward/*] *ward* interlined in darker ink 2338 *acqu<~~a~~>‸\a/inted*] <~~a~~> blotted; replaced by interlined *a*; caret below <~~a~~> 2339 *his*] *s* possibly altered from *m* 2345] SP high 2347 <~~.n~~>] smeared for deletion 2348 *tric\k/~~k~~*] ²*k* blotted; replaced by interlined *k*

ing ony mon an answer that shall ask why he did so.
Alb: When a mans own faults draw him into danger
Tis fitt his guiltie head should vndergoe
The punishment his foule offences call for.

[FOL. 225v/30v]

And since I cannot cleare me of disgrace
'Tis comfort but to hope to lessen it,
I'le follow yor direction, & in that shape
Hazard my selfe.
Zep: And I will prsently send for the beares skin. *Ex. Ambo.*

Enter Caguirino, Lisetta, Bergamino, Landolpho, Oretta, Dianora, Rinaldo, & Obedience. [Act 5, scene iv]

Cag: No sooner had I disingag'd my selfe
Of the imposition wch the state layd on me,
By declaration of their appointed pleasure
Conteined in the embassie I carried,
But my soule quit of feare began to weigh
My sorrow causd in missing you, yet hoping
The carefull vigilancie wch I had
In those great things I was intrusted wth
Had purchas'd heaun's fauour so farr that I
Might once more see you, my duty & the states
Impose discharg'd, the swiftnes of my thoughts
Sayld faster then the ship, & was here long
Before I saw the land.
Lis: Happier newes
My longing eare was nere acquainted wth
Then when the wellcome sailers made relation
Of yor desired safetie & returne.
Ber: And if you'l creditt but the testimonie
Of me that scorne to giue you information
Of any thing but truth; I can assure you
More pensiuenes did neuer seize a woman
To fill her thoughts wth sadnes, then extremitie
Of greefe occasion'd by yor mourn'd for absence
Surpris'd my sister.

2357 *draw*] *d* altered   2370 *in*] *n* possibly altered

Cag: My strong beleefe
Will not be so iniurious as to question
Yo^{r} words or her indear'd affection.

Dia. If all women were like her they must ether trauell
wth their husbands, if they should goe to stay but one
weeke from home, or els they would be in great danger
of falling into a consumption.

Oret. Indeed we thought to haue put vp a petition, that a ship
might haue bene prest to haue carried her after yo^{u}, for
she did so pule & cry, that if it had not bene for good aduise
& merry company, she had before now rather needed an epitaph
then a husband.

31. [FOL. 226r]

Ob: I M^{r}, if yo^{u} had but heard her grones, & sighes, & sobbs
that she fetcht, & how in the night she threw her ~~leggs~~ \arms/
one way, & her ~~armes~~ \leggs/ another, yo^{u} would haue thought
she had bene ridden wth the night mare, As I am a
true virgin, I would haue morgag'd my tiffanie ruffe
that I weare on holy dayes, & my shadow wth the cutt=
work edging to haue had her well againe.

Cag All these are the infallible demonstrations
Of her pure loue & my vnualued happines,
In thankfullnes whereof & plaine expression
Of my thoughts secret ioy, this night wee'l spend
In fresh reuiuing those delicious plesures
Absence hath wth an enuious cessation
Barr'd me from tasting.

Rin. 'Pray since all's well as may be,
Let me obtaine that *Obedience* & I
May lye ith' next roome to yo^{u} for we are maried,
And though we cannot eccho yo^{u} in kissing
For want of practise, wee'l vault as high as yo^{u},
And if it be not a stout hearted bed=cord
Venture to make the fether bed fall thorough.

Cag. Yo^{u} shall, & I will doe thee a greater fauour
Then this, for thou shalt haue the keeping of
The lodge & park I bought of my lord what de' call.

2394] SP high

Rin. I humbly thank yo^{u} S^{r}, & hope yo^{u} will not
Be offended if ‸\my wife/ for the good conuenience
Of weekely taking mony, ~~we~~ haue curds
And creame as in hide parke, & nurse a child
There <.> of a citisens wifes, wch she dare~~st~~ not
~~Haue bred ith' citty~~
Be known t' haue bred ith' citty 'cause 'twas gott
In that dead hungry time when her husband last
was at East Indies.
Cag: I promise yo^{u} I will not.
Rin: Well then Ile weare as good clothes as an aldermans
son.
Cag. Yo^{r} own imagination needs must tell yo^{u}
I stand on thorns vntill I be in bed;
Nor will I stay till it be night, for things
Deferrd sometimes doe cause the appetite
To die; but if you'l please to morow dinner
To grace o^{r} table, wth yor company

[FOL. 226v/31v]

I think the foole rides my m^{r}, if he knew how little
would serue him, he would take time & do't better, he's old
& yong, an old maried man, & a boy in appetite, he's full
as hot o the quarry as a ward that's matchd before he come
to yeares of consent & would fayne be pidling.
And these two gentlewomen vouchafe to come,
Wee'l drink a health to the boy I get to night
And another to the company yo^{u} daign'd
To afford her in my absence, till then farewell. *Ex: Cag. & Lisett*
Oret. I neuer did deny an inuitation
That was so kindly made, we will not faile. *Ex: Or. & Dia*
Rin. Thou & I will not be so hasty, we haue done thou
knowest what so often before we were maried, that we
can afford to stay now till we haue had all the solemni=
ties, the fidlers & the sack posset, & so goe to't in temper
& get children wth discretion.

2431 <.>] smeared or blotted *dare~~st~~*] ~~*st*~~ smeared for deletion and *e* inserted 2432] smeared for deletion 2451a–e] five additional lines preceded by a trefoil symbol and written in a slightly darker ink in the top margin; marked for insertion with the same trefoil symbol at l. 2451 after the SP and before the start of the line

Ob: Pray let's ha' one bout ith' landrie before night.
Enter friar Ricciardo, & friar Adrian.
Ricc. Although it be an auncient vsed custome
For men of o^{r} profession to walke abroad
By two & two together, & so return
Home to the conuent like a holy paire;
Yet because o^{r} brother *Alberts* great occasions
Detein'd him longer in the towne then I
Could well stay wth him, by reason of an exercise
I am shortly to performe before the *Nuntio*
His holines sends hither, I made bold
To leaue him in this place, & since that time
I neuer saw him nor heard word of him.
Enter Zeppa & a Bellman.
Rin. If he were not a friar, yo^{u} might sweare he were kill'd
in a baudie house, for that's as vsuall now as to hang
a dog for hawkesmeat. *The friars walk.*
Zeppa takes Bergamino & Landolpho aside.
Zep: Wun ye le me speake wi yo^{u}, he has told me all the
matter himselfe, & is as fearefull as a courst hare, so I ha'
ꝑswaded him to put on a beares skin, & in that disguise
he is now ready to come forth, in great good hope to
scape, now if yo^{u} think good yo^{u} may pull of his visor, w^{ch}
hee'l take as discourteously as if yo^{u} should wipe a painted
Ladies face wth a weet handcarcheife, & disgrace him as
much as if yo^{u} should pull of a gentlewomans false haire,
(for these two things a cha^\u/mbermaid told me but will<e> greeue
a ~~gentle~~woman more then her fathers death) and to
make him more asham'd I haue brought the bellman,
who shall make a dinn, & proclaime that here will p^{r}sently
be a strange beast to be seene, & that will draw such a ~~com~~=
32. [Fol. 227r]
company, & so great crouds of people together that
they will laugh him out of his skin.
Lan: It will doe very well, & that will be all the reuenge
we can take of him, for here are two of the same order,
& we may not offer any open violence to him, when
they are by, but it will be full as good for them
to see him in such a habit, as if all the dirt in the

kennell were thrown vpon him.

Zep: Then Ile bid the bellman make proclamation.

Lan: I pray doe.

Zep: Cry the streue & see if any man will owne him.

Bellman All manner of persons that desire [*rings thrice then speaks.*]
to see a god transform'd into a man, & a man into
a beast, such as *Africa* or *Asia* neuer bred, nor *Pliny*
nor *Topsell* euer describ'd, let them be here presently
& they shall see the monster appeare in his likenes.

Ricc: What strange proclamation is this? [*Ex: Zep: & Belman.*]

Lan: You shall see what it meanes incontinently, for he that
keepes the beast will bring him forth p^{r}sently, & they
say he's a learned beast, for all the beginning of his
life he was brought vp in a monasterie, & as his keeꝑ
tells me he was a great companion of frier *Alberts*,
whom yo^{u} say yo^{u} miss.

Ricc: Yes truly, & all the brothers of the conuent
Haue nam'd a day to solemnize the rites
Of his appointed funerall, vnles
In the interim they haue some certaine notice
He is aliue & well.

Lan: To quitt yor care
Of such obseruance to a man so base
I'm bound to striue, That villan is a liue
And breathes, but when yor knowledge shall partake
Of his black sins shrouded in robes of goodnes,
The duty wch yo^{u} owe to heau'n & Iustice
Cannot forbeare to wreake the iniuries
He hath offered yo^{u} & vs & all good men,
And to reward him I am sure yo^{u} will
Spitt vengeance in his face from yor iust mouthes.

Adria. Yo^{r} implication is so intricate
We cannot vnderstand it, nor may we suffer
A contumely to be vniustly laid
Vpon a holy brother.

[Fol. 227v/32v]

2498 *rings… /speaks*] SD written in R margin; ink line indicates intended point of insertion before l. 2498 2517 *a liue*] = *aliue*

Rin. These two gentlemen
My m^{ris} brothers hide their iniurie
As much as may be, & I that euer haue bene
Seruant to their dispose can right them so farr
They haue not laid a wrong taxation on him.
Ber: It will appeare the slaue's asham'd to be
Seene as a man, the sequell will explaine
What I inferr obscurely. *Enter Albert like a beare led by Zeppa.*
Zep: Here comes a sober beast 'pray
make him roome.
Rin: Is this he that was a man once?
Zep: Yes.
Ob: I cannot abide a beare of all things ith' world, especi=
ally at this time, for they say, if a beare should chance to break
loose he will euer come to a woman wth child, & though
I haue bene so little a while married, yet if I had not
cause to suspect my selfe wth child, I were not worthy
to haue that trust repos'd in me wch most chambermaids
haue, & that is the~~<e>~~ keeping of their m^{ris} complexion ~~box~~
box, & so mirth be at yor sport *About to goe* .
Rin. Stay sweet pug, one kiss before thou goest, *they kiss*
Now goe when thou wilt but against night be sure
to haue the warming pan ready; for I am like a iaded
courtier that ha's lost the calues of his leggs in the
not y^{is} Ladies seruice, & now needs a pan of coles or some of
My Lo: of Lecesters water to help erection..
Ob: That concerns me to looke to, & besides the warming
pan Ile prouide thee burnt ale wth eggs. *Exit Ob:*
Adri: It fitts not wth o^{r} grauitie to stay
To see such idle sports, but since yor enuie,
I know not how procur'd, hath wrongfully
Tax'd o^{r} deceased brother, we're bound to cleare
Him of all ill aspersions.
Ber: Yo^{u} cannot doe't.
Adri: Declare yor selues in plaine words, I assure yo^{u}
We will not put this wrong vp, & if yo^{u} doe not

2539] SP high   2547 *the<e>*] <e> smeared for deletion

Giue a good reason for what yo^{u} haue said allready
Yo^{u} shall be curst wth bell booke & candle.
Ber: I am content, & if it doe appeare
Albert is here in person yet dare not shew
Himselfe but in disguise, I hope you'l change

33. [Fol. 228r]

The misopinion yo^{u} conceaue of vs
And giue him his desert.
Ricc. 'Tis fitt we should.
Lan: Will yo^{u} afford vs but the courtesie
Onely to stay till the beare hath done one trick.
Ricc: yes that we will.
Lan. Yo^{u} bind vs to yo^{u} then, *Zeppa* make yor beare stand.
Zep: He wun not stand, nor neuer wud sin he lost his eeres.
Rin. How did he loose his eares?
Zep: When he was a mon, he was wone while o wone pro=
fession, & otherwhiles of another, he was otherwhiles
a pettiefogger & otherwhiles an atturnye, & when he
was an atturnye he was set o' th' pillory for forging
a l‸\y/ease, & there he lost his eeres.
Rin: Good m^{r} Atturny here's ten groats for yo^{u} S^{r} [*strikes him on the head*]
Zep. O — doe not strike him so hard, a beare ~~ho~~
ha's the thinnest scull, but we call't a scawp, the thinnest
scawp or scull wch yo' wun of ony creature liuing, & if
ye should chance to crack it, yo^{u} wud both indaunger
his life, & poyson yor own fingers, if ony othe brenes
should fortune to fly out by casultie, for a beares
brenes are as ronk poyson as an atturnies, & euer
haue bene since he was an atturnie.
Rin. Good m^{r} atturny, I cry yor vndershreeueship mercy
S^{r}, I am sure yo^{u} ha' bene one in yor dayes.
Lan: Cannot yo^{u} make yor beare stand?
Zep: In sadnes I connot, I wud make him stand if I
cou'd, Hy Harry Hy, Hy Harry Hy ://. [*Beare reares & stands.*]
Adr: The beast is very docible if he had
but a good keeper. [*Beare falls againe*]

2578] SP high 2598] SP high

Zep: He connot stond lung, nothing that has bene so
much among wemen in's youth as he has bene
con stond lung.
Rin. He was not a gentleman vsher, was he?
Zep: No but he was a great beater of bucks.
Lan: He has bene twenty things it seemes, was he
neuer a friar? *Beare grumbles.*
Zep. In sadnes I know not, but Ile tell yo^{u} p^{r}sently, he
can heare & vnderstand very well, but he cannot
aunser but by signes, & when yo^{u} ask him a question
if he answer you I, he do's thus, if no grunts claps his
futt on his breech, & runs back. Were yo^{u} euer a frier?
Beare doth the negatiue action.

[Fol. 228v/33v]

Ber: It may be his hearing's bad ask him againe.
Zep: O no his hearing is exceeding good, but he hath
no mind to answer, were yo^{u} euer a friar? *Beare runs back & grumbles*
Ricc: Yo^{u} trouble the poore dumb thing, let him alone.
Ber: Ile but ask him once my selfe, & if he doe
not answer then, Ile trouble him no more, some
body lend me a great pin or a bodkin; oh now
I think on't, (according to the gallants garb) I
haue a paire of tweeses in my pocket that will
yeeld me a sufficient weapon, *takes the tweeses & out of them pulls a bodkin*
Come on S^{r}, if yo^{u} cannot speake
Ile make you roare. *He pricks him wth the bodkin.*
Is yor feeling bad to? *The beare runs back, then round.*
Alb: S^{t} francis execration light vpon you.
Lan: Nay if yo^{u} speake weel see yor cursed face *plucks of the visor*
A friar, A friar, a friar, &c:
Ber: An *Albert*, an *Albert*, an *Albert*. &c. *All the foure continue*
Rin: A friar an *Albert*, an *Albert* a friar. &c. *speaking together*
Zep: A *Cupid*, a *Cupid*, a *Cupid* ——— &c. *then all shout*
They shout. *viz: Landolpho, Bergamino, Rinaldo, & Zeppa.*
Adri: Cease this vnruly outcrie, & giue account
Why yo^{u} disturb o^{r} eares & fill the aire
Wth this ~~a~~ outragious sound.

2606 *grumbles*] altered from *grunts* after SD was boxed for deletion 2610 *answer*] *we* altered 2635 ~~*a*~~] smeared

Ber: This is the man yo^{u} mist? 'pray is it not?
Ricc: Yes & we're glad to see him
Ber: You'l make good
Yo^{r} word I hope wch was if friar *Albert*
Durst not in his own person shew his face
We might be cleared from the hard conceipt
Yo^{u} had of vs & his head beare the punishment
His fault deserues.
Adri: We do not vnderstand
He's guilty yet of any hainous sin.
Lan: ~~I know you'l doe both vs & him iust right~~
~~And then we shall be satisfied, this villaine~~
~~W^{ch} epithet his sin hath giu'n him~~
~~Is a most irreligious foule adulterer~~
~~And in a faire p^{r}tence of holines~~
~~Hath iniur'd & defil'd a married wife.~~
Ricc: ~~You doe miscall him, he is no adulterer~~.

34. [Fol. 229r]

Alb: My silence speakes my crime, & I confesse
My guiltines deserues the fruit of sin
W^{ch} is disgrace & punishment, yet what the mulct
Shall be for my offence, yo^{u} must determine
And not lay peoples hasty condemnation.
Lan: I know you'l doe both vs & him iust right
And then we shall be satisfied, this villaine
(W^{ch} epithet his sin hath giu'n him)
Is a most irreligious foule adulterer
And in a faire p^{r}tence of holines
Hath iniur'd & defil'd a married wife
Ricc: Yo^{u} doe miscall him he is no adulterer.
Lan: He hath layn wth her.
Ricc: 'Pray what if he haue?
Lan: I therefore craue he may be banished
At least expelled yor sacred house & order.
Adri: We cannot grant yor suite, nor may we doe this
O^{r} statutes giue such freedome, & in him

2646–52] deleted with criss-crossing ink lines; text relocated to ll. 2658–64 2666 *'Pray*] followed by a hooked superscript pen stroke, possibly false start for a *?*

This act cannot be calld adulterie
But *simplex fornicatio*, & for that
He cannot loose his place, for we're allow'd
This priuiledge, that no man shall be expell'd
Nisi propter crebram fornicationem
And what *crebra fornicatio* is
O^{r} own brests must determine & not yo^{r}ꞇ.

Ber: And is this the greatest satisfaction
An iniur'd man can get from yor iniustice?

Alb: The ~~<g>~~ cheefest remedie I know is to be quiet
And drown yor greefe in *Lethe*.

Lan: Farewell friars,
You'u're gods in shew but deuillish fiends in action [*Ex. Lan: & Ber:*]

Rin. × How happy are the friars that may doe thus. [*Exit.*]

Zep: Honest beare farewell I am sure I ha' got most by thee. [*Ex: Ze:*]

Adri: 'Tis an high point of pollicie to make
The com̃on people feare; & to perswade
Them that it is damnation to denie [not y^{is}]
Any thing we affirme.

Alb: That course I hold
And confidently told her I made vse of
She could not merit but in pleasing me
Which her obliged conscience did beleeue

[FOL. 229V/34V]

Because I said it, & this easie way
I gaind my ends wch her durst not say nay. [*Ex: Ões.*]

Epilogue.

If yor vneasie seats haue tyr'd yo^{u} so
You're glad to leaue 'hem, there's none of yo^{u} but know
That haue a child, yo^{u} loue to see it clipt
In Dandling armes, & if the authour slipt
Into a fault, because his actiue pen
Begott this child, & 'tis the loue of men
To wish their heires long=liu'd, he hopes you'l please
T' excuse his errour, wch is a disease
Of loue to his own ofspring, & so ties

2680 ~~<g>~~] smeared for deletion

Him to be thus indulgent. If yor eies
Be weary as yor eares & other parts
Yo^{u} may release 'hem, & crown o^{r} deserts
    If yor applausiue hands vouchafe to shew
    Yo^{u} grace the authour, as he honours yo^{u}.

Exit.